RARE BIRDS

RARE BIRDS

JEFF MILLER

union
square
kids

NEW YORK

TO MY MOTHER.
AND TO THE PERSON WHO GAVE US THE GIFT OF LIFE.
WE ARE FOREVER GRATEFUL.

**union
square
kids**

NEW YORK

UNION SQUARE KIDS and the distinctive Union Square Kids
logo are trademarks of Union Square & Co., LLC.

Union Square & Co., LLC, is a subsidiary of Sterling Publishing Co., Inc.

Text © 2023 Alloy Entertainment, LLC
Cover illustration © 2023 Kimberly Glyder

Produced by Alloy Entertainment

ISBN 978-1-4549-4504-8
ISBN 978-1-4549-4506-2 (e-book)

Library of Congress Cataloging-in-Publication Data

Names: Miller, Jeff R., author.
Title: Rare birds / Jeff Miller.
Description: [New York] : Union Square Kids, [2023] | Audience: Ages 8-12.
  | Audience: Grades 4-6. | Summary: While his mother waits for a
  life-saving heart transplant, eleven-year-old Graham Dodds sets out to
  find an endangered Snail Kite in the Florida Everglades.
Identifiers: LCCN 2022002466 | ISBN 9781454945048 (hardcover) | ISBN
  9781454945062 (e-book)
Subjects: CYAC: Birds--Fiction. | Endangered species--Fiction. |
  Heart--Transplantation--Fiction. | Families--Fiction. | Everglades
  (Fla.)--Fiction. | Florida--Fiction. | BISAC: JUVENILE FICTION / Social
  Themes / Adolescence & Coming of Age | JUVENILE FICTION / Health & Daily
  Living / Diseases, Illnesses & Injuries | LCGFT: Fiction. | Novels.
Classification: LCC PZ7.M61815 Rar 2023 | DDC [Fic]--dc23
LC record available at https://lccn.loc.gov/2022002466

For information about custom editions, special sales, and premium purchases,
please contact specialsales@unionsquareandco.com.

Printed in the U.S.A.

Lot #:
2 4 6 8 10 9 7 5 3 1

11/22

unionsquareandco.com

Cover design by Kimberly Glyder
Interior design by Julie Robine

My Waiting Room

Brains are weird, right?

I can be sitting here in seat 25A of this airplane, surrounded by strangers and my mom, and if I close my eyes, I can be transported to a totally different place.

In a split second I can go somewhere breathtaking, like the top of the world's tallest mountain. Or the sandy, sunburnt valley of the hottest desert. Or . . . Buffalo, New York! Where my favorite restaurant of all time serves the world's best broccoli cheddar soup bread bowl. Brains even allow you to go to each amazing spot all at once. I can see myself now, up on top of the tallest mountain . . . overlooking the planet's hottest desert . . . lounging in a hot-tub sized bread bowl.

Okay, okay, the soup part would be gross, but you get the idea.

The truth is, even though my brain could take me magical places, it spends most of its time in one place. I call it My Waiting Room.

Welcome.

I come here whenever I'm feeling not-quite-bored and not-quite-lonely and not-quite-sad. It's the place my imagination carries me to whenever I'm feeling . . . "in between," which is a lot these days.

Now that you're here with me, let me show you around.

In many ways My Waiting Room is just like one you'd find in every other hospital: It has the same vending machines filled with old candy nobody ever buys, the same uncomfortable chairs that constantly wobble, and the same stacks of old magazines. Oh, and there's a TV that never plays anything good.

There are also two doors.

Behind one door is a miracle. And behind the other door is a disaster.

A disastrous disaster.

That's the crummy thing about hospital waiting rooms: you're only ever in them to see which type of news you're about to get. Either way your life is going to be changed forever. My job is to wait.

And wait.

And wait.

And waaaiiittt.

And let me tell you, it's not easy to wait to see if your mom is going to live or die.

I feel my ears begin to adjust to a change in pressure, so I open my eyes. I'm back in seat 25A, flying from Buffalo to Miami. Like I said, brains are weird.

Next Destination

"Ladies and gentlemen, we are beginning our final descent."

My stomach lurches looking out the window as we make a wide turn over the glimmering ocean. Swamps and houses and swimming pools grow closer until I can almost make out the ant-size people lounging around them.

"Local time in Miami is 7:52 p.m. on this first day of June, with a temperature of eighty-eight degrees. Now we know y'all can choose anyone to fly with, so from everyone on the flight crew—"

"Thank you for flying with us, and we'll see you next time," I say along with the pilot.

I've pretty much got the whole boarding and deboarding routine memorized start to finish. Sometimes the flight crew will give suggestions about where to go in your new destination, too. In Buffalo, they tell you the best places to order chicken wings. In Seattle, it's the best place to get a fresh fish thrown at you really, really hard. Everything else stays the same, though.

My mom nudges me with her elbow. She points out the window at the beach below. It looks just like the pictures I've seen on my mapping app—a road of sand and sunshine that runs the length of Florida, blue water practically lapping at its shoreline. I can almost see the sunburns and drinks with frilly umbrellas.

"Is that mini-golf course you worked at down there somewhere?" I ask, peering down at the road dotted with beaches.

"Oh, I think they tore that down a while ago. I bet it's a restaurant or a doctor's office now," she replies, leaning back into her seat. "Those summers were the best. Me and Dom would spend twenty bucks on arcade games trying to win fake sunglasses. We called them *Roy-Bons*," Mom says with a chuckle.

The plane makes a sharp turn and my stomach drops.

"And who exactly is Dom again?" I say, turning to her. "I usually like to know a guy before hopping in his van. Can never be too careful."

Mom laughs, pulling her hair to one side.

"You'll love him. We grew up together here in Sugarland."

The landing gear unfolds and the plane touches down with a few soft bounces. This is officially the fourth city we've been to since my tenth birthday, the day it all started.

We were in Chicago when we rushed to the hospital in the back of an ambulance, my ice cream cake still in the freezer. It was the first time I saw her like that, scared and surrounded by wires and machines. From Chicago we went to Seattle, then Minneapolis for, like, three months. And finally to Buffalo, for most of last year, which was actually cool. Mom and I both made friends there, which made it harder to leave.

Each new place is exactly the same, with new doctors and surgeons and hospital officials saying they have got the answer to all our problems. Well, my mom's problems. I'm just along for the ride.

They've always got the *best* doctors or the *newest* hospitals or most *cutting-edge* treatments. Only none of them have worked. After all this moving around, we're still no closer to a cure. So far, we only have a diagnosis: dilated cardiomyopathy. (It took a while to learn how to spell it.)

Basically, it's where somebody's heart gets very sick and can barely do what it needs to do to keep them alive. Then, when it's too tired, it starts beating out of control. Like, so out of control that it could kill you.

The only way to stop that is to blast somebody in the chest with those paddles you see on TV shows. My mom has a device inside of her that does the blasting, so she doesn't need somebody standing around shouting *"clear!"*

But the doctors down here in Florida? They say they've got an answer. They say that since her heart is failing, she needs a new one—a transplant—and that it's our only option left.

This time I might believe them. Because if a new heart won't fix my mom, I don't know what will.

Mom says once we leave here, and she's all better, we can finally go home—whichever home we want that to be. (I want it to be Buffalo.)

"Here we go, G," says Mom as the airplane crawls to a stop on the runway. "It all happens for a reason."

I slip my hand into my mom's and squeeze it.

HALF THE BATTLE

I KNOW WHAT YOU'RE THINKING. YOU'RE THINKING THAT IT STINKS TO move around a lot. And it stinks to leave your friends behind. And it stinks to have a mom who's sick. You might even be saying, "Wow, Graham, does your life always stink?"

And, I don't know, maybe you're right?

But if you tell my mom that her life stinks, she'll just tell you: "It all happens for a reason."

Like most coaches for professional sports, my mom believes in the power of a good saying. A motto. A mantra. So that's why she'll say "it all happens for a reason" roughly three hundred billion times a day.

Her doctors have their own sayings, like "hang in there, slugger" and "being positive is half the battle."

But sometimes I want to scream: "What about the other half?"

I know what happens on the other half of the battle, and I can tell you no one has any sayings over there.

Anyways.

I'm trying to stay positive. I promise.

WELCOME TO SUGARLAND

"IT'S GOING TO WORK THIS TIME, GRAHAMY," SHE TELLS ME AS THE SEATBELT light turns off with a *ding*. Everyone around us stands up, reaching for carry-on items and picking their wedgies.

I nod. Just the thought of somebody cutting into me and, like, replacing my pinkie nail gives me chills. But a heart?

"Remember that afternoon in Seattle, when we first left the hospital?" Mom asks.

"When there was basically a monsoon out of nowhere and we had to walk half a mile to our car?" I reply.

"Exactly. And we started to run, and we were soaked and cold. But then we just started laughing," she says with a smile. "And we jumped in every puddle we saw."

"And then that Golden Eagle swooped right over us and landed on the roof of our car!" I say, the memory coming back vividly. "If my phone wasn't totally soaked, I would've had the best photo ever. I can still remember the sparkling gold flecks in its brown eyes."

"Seeing what others don't. Your superpower." Mom chuckles.

Not to brag, but I'm pretty good at noticing little details that might slip past other people. Like when a pet dog looks exactly like their owner, or when somebody doesn't remember words to a song and tries to mumble along without someone else hearing (I always do). This weirdly helps in getting photos of birds, too.

My mom loves, and I mean LOVES, bird-watching. She never takes their pictures, though, no matter how rare the bird. She believes birds are, like, spirits who have passed away, and each one is coming to say hello. She never wants to scare them off. Some real mom stuff, if you ask me.

We step into the crowded airplane aisle and shuffle forward. "That day in Seattle is a good reminder, G, that sometimes when life is nothing but puddles, you—"

"End up with a bird of prey on top of your sedan?" I joke. And I don't know why, but this makes us both crack up. And once we start, it's hard to stop. My mom is really good at that. The flight attendant smiles at us as we pass. Her nametag says *Lindsay*—same as my mom's name.

"Did you see that? It all happens—"

"Mom, you're reaching your limit for the day," I say as we step off the plane.

"—for a reason." Mom smiles. The humidity surrounds us like the hot breath from a dog. "Welcome to Sugarland."

THE BLUE BEAST

THE RADIO OF DOM'S ANCIENT, FADED BLUE VAN IS PLAYING A TOM PETTY song full-blast—he's one of my mom's favorites, so I've heard it before. Every window is down, and my mom's hair is whipping around her face as she sings along. It's like the mom I knew has suddenly gotten a factory reset and is once again a seventeen-year-old.

Kachunk!

The van hits a pothole and I grip the door handle super tight. The entire vehicle feels like it might fall into pieces at any given moment.

I'm behind Dom, sharing the back-bench seat with a stack of paintbrushes, a warm energy drink, and a handful of CDs by a group called "Crosby, Stills, Nash, and Young." The name sounds like a group of lawyers or orthodontists.

"I can't believe this van still works," Mom says, running a hand over the vehicle's faded dashboard. "I'm pretty sure you drove me to high school in this thing."

"The Blue Beast," Dom says from the driver's seat, his arm out the window. He pats the side of the door like he would a beloved pet. "Still runnin' like a top."

Dom has a toothpick in the corner of his mouth and is wearing a white T-shirt and paint-splattered white overalls. His forearm hair is speckled with multicolored paint drops. He looks like a man-size Easter egg.

"So how have you been, Dom? What's new?" my mom asks.

"Oh, you know me, same dirt, different shirt," Dom answers as he eyes the rearview mirror in his bulky silver sunglasses—the kind that are only worn by outfielders and fishermen. "I hear you're turnin' twelve end of this summer, Graham. You play any sports or anything?" he asks.

"Soccer, I guess," I reply.

"Graham was going to try out for the team back in Buffalo before we left," Mom adds from the passenger seat.

"Nice," Dom says. "This your first time to Florida, then?"

"First time I remember being here, at least."

"Graham wasn't even two years old when we moved to Chicago," Mom says.

I'm pretty sure the earliest memory I have is of me and my mom dipping the back tires of our car into Lake Michigan once we got there—she said it was tradition. Apparently, my dad used to do that before and after every trip. I just remember being really excited (and also nervous that we might get stuck).

"Your dad was a good man," Dom says, almost like he's reading my mind. "A real good guy."

"Thanks," I say.

My dad died when I was one and a half. Everyone says he was a good guy. Such a good guy that he died trying to save some people during a hurricane. Sometimes I secretly wish he was a less good guy and a more alive guy.

But mostly thinking about my dad just makes me extra glad I've got my mom. We're all each other's got.

I look out to see the clouds turn shades of pink and blue. I don't know why, but the soapy hues make me feel calm. As though it's the sun's way of telling us everything is going to be okay—that maybe Sugarland is the miracle we've been waiting for.

GATORS

"HOME SWEET HOME," DOM SAYS AS WE PULL ONTO A LONG GRAVEL ROAD that winds through gnarly, old-looking trees. Their huge, crooked branches are covered with stringy moss and loom over us. We eventually exit the slightly spooky tree tunnel and stop in front of a freshly painted ranch house. It's small, and besides the new coat of light-yellow paint, it seems like nothing about it has been changed in decades. Ivy is growing up the side of the stone chimney, and the address numbers on the red front door are cracked and splintered from years of sun.

Behind the house is a perfectly trimmed lawn that's surrounded by wild swampland. Twisted trees poke out in all directions, trying to overtake the wooden fences marking the border of the yard.

Dom pushes the garage door controller on the visor. After a pause, the white wooden garage door gently creaks open. A calico cat runs out from a bush next to the garage, briefly mewing before darting off.

"For the record, everybody—that cat is a liar. Don't ever trust it," Dom says, turning off the van in the driveway as the garage door finishes opening. "And be alert, Graham. Gotta keep an eye out for the gators."

My palms sweat. "Gators?"

"Oh, you probably won't see any," Dom says with a wink. "Probably."

"Wait, *seriously*?" I shout.

But he and my mom are already stepping into the garage.

AN UN-WHALE-COME STRANGER

I SIT FOR A FEW SECONDS, GAZING AT THE TANGLED WILDERNESS TWENTY yards away. I remind myself there's probably not a family of hungry swamp monsters waiting for me. There totally, definitely isn't.

Totally.

Definitely.

I take a deep breath and hop out of the van.

I walk into the garage where a lightbulb is buzzing overhead, revealing a museum of old ladders and fishing poles. Dom starts emptying his van of paint cans and drop cloths, piling it next to boxes with "Lindsay" scrawled on their side.

"Oh, Dom, I didn't realize it was so much stuff!" Mom says, looking at the mountain of boxes from my grandma's old place. She moved out West to live with my aunt a few years ago, when she couldn't really take care of herself anymore. Dom's been holding on to Mom's stuff since then. "We can get this sorted right away."

She walks over to one of the boxes, unfolds the flaps, and begins to sift through.

"I didn't know what you'd want to hang on to, so I just saved it all," Dom says. "Your mom really had a thing for whales, huh?"

I watch my mom reach into a cardboard box and pull out a sign in the shape of a whale making a winky face. *Whale-Come to Our Home*, it reads. "Wow, I haven't seen some of this stuff in years and years."

"Well, it'll still be there tomorrow. Let's go see what we've got to fix up for dinner," Dom tells her.

"You know what I've been craving?" Mom says. "Swansen's."

Dom laughs. "I'm sure you have. In high school you couldn't go three days without going there."

"What's Swansen's?" I ask.

"Swansen's is only the best place in the world, Graham Dodds," Mom says. "Just imagine a burger with the ultimate secret recipe sauce. A chocolate peanut butter shake that's impossible to drink with a straw. A bag full of fries that's so greasy you can see right through it."

I nod my head. These are all impressive food groups.

"Then it's settled. Swansen's it is!" Mom says with glee. "For you guys, at least. My doctors probably get alerts whenever I'm within fifty feet of a hamburger."

"We can at least sneak you a few fries, Linds. I'll come with, but you're in charge of the Blue Beast from here on," Dom says as he tosses my mom the keys. "It's a nice night for a ride. You comin', Graham?"

A breeze of warm Florida air rushes around us. Even after the sun sets it's somehow still hot.

"Actually, would you mind if I hung out here and took a shower?"

"Course not. There's a towel on your bed, Graham," Dom says. "Tell Nick to call in the order. We can do the family combo, with a veggie wrap for your mom."

I tilt my head, confused. "Wait, who's Nick?" I ask.

"Nick's my boy, about your age, too," Dom says. "Tell him I said to turn off the TV and show you around."

"Oh. Cool," I reply. I shoot a quick, perplexed glance at my mom. She didn't tell me that Dom had a son. Why would she leave that out?

She just grins at me, as though to say, "Isn't this the best surprise ever?!"

I widen my eyes back, as though to say, "Not really."

"Go in through the back. You'll see a sliding glass door around the garage," Dom says with a pointed finger.

Mom gets behind the wheel of the van.

"You sure I can drive this thing?" she asks.

"You're fine. You just gotta give it the business to get it started," Dom says. Mom gives it some gas and it roars to life. She gives the engine a few quick revs with an electric smile.

"We'll be right back, Graham," she says.

"Have fun," I reply, with only a touch of sarcasm. I add a thumbs-up for good measure. Staying positive.

Technically.

AND SON

"Hey, Dad," says a voice from nowhere, as I step into the sparsely decorated living room. Two leather recliners face a giant TV. A blue couch is pushed all the way into the corner and seems to be used as more of a coatrack/mailbox. The TV is playing a professional wrestling match.

"Hey. I'm Graham," I say over the sounds of body slams. "Are you Nick? Your dad told me to ask you to order the family meal. At Swansen's?"

A recliner spins around and Nick stares back at me. He's a little chubby and has a buzz cut that's growing out. He's very tan and wearing a faded T-shirt that says *Dom and Son Painting* in cursive writing.

"So, you're the person who's sharing my room then," he says. From his scowl, it seems he isn't happy about it.

"Huh. I guess I didn't realize I was sharing a room with anybody. That's, ah, cool, though," I say. Most everywhere we've been, the hospitals have helped set us up with a two-bedroom apartment, so I'm not exactly used to the idea of a roommate.

"Just don't touch any of my stuff, and stay out of my way," Nick says, pulling out his phone.

"No prob," I assure him. "And my mom wants a veggie wrap. I'll take a burger plain—I hate mustard and mayo."

I listen as Nick places the order for pickup. He talks using very few words, saying "okay" and "family meal for four" over and over to the person on the other end of the call.

"We'll take a veggie wrap, too, and make sure there's extra mayo and mustard on all the burgers. Thanks," Nick says as he ends the call and walks into the bathroom.

I sigh, rolling my eyes to the bumpy-looking ceiling.

Nick is a bully. Got it.

I know about bullies.

The first week we lived in Seattle they had that day where parents come in and talk about their jobs, but my mom was stuck in the hospital. She came in a week later and did a presentation on her full-time job: getting better. She borrowed a bunch of stuff from the hospital including an IV bag and stethoscope. It was pretty cool. But after that, the guys in my class started calling me Patient Zero.

I glance around the rest of the house. It looks . . . stuck in time. Like nobody's done anything to it in years. There aren't any family photos or anything, and all the carpet is shaggy and lime green. I walk toward the kitchen, briefly looking down the dark hallway that I figure leads to the bedrooms.

The kitchen floor is covered with old multicolored tiles, and there are a couple of bags of recycling filling up in the corner. The counter is covered with empty doughnut boxes and it all smells like old coffee. The stove is huge and white and looks more like an incinerator than something to cook with—same with the fridge. They both look like they might run off coal or steam or whatever was used in the 1800s.

Nick lumbers into the kitchen, opens the refrigerator, and pours himself a glass of orange juice.

"I hear you're sick," he says, slugging back his juice. He wipes his mouth with the back of his hand.

"I'm not actually sick. It's my mom."

"Oh," says Nick. Even barefoot he's about three inches taller than me. He leaves his glass on the counter.

"Mind if I go to your room?" I ask, changing the subject. "I need to put down my backpack and charge my phone."

"Down the hall, the last door on the right. I'm going to finish my show," he says, returning to his chair. "You know my dad's really helping you guys out, you being so in the way and everything."

I feel my stomach drop. I hate feeling like I'm in anybody's way.

"What do you mean?" I ask and clear my throat.

"I just don't see why we have to be the ones suffering," Nick says before turning the volume on the TV back up.

I head toward my new bedroom but turn back toward Nick after a few steps. "Maybe we'll be helping you guys out. The kitchen might get cleaned for once," I say over the wrestling commentators.

"What?" Nick says from his recliner.

Staying positive.

"Nothing," I mumble as I continue to the bedroom.

I step inside and shut the door. There's an old army cot with a

University of Florida Gators comforter perched in the corner. I lie down on it, shutting my eyes. I let my thoughts drift away to My Waiting Room, and I remind myself this is what has to be done to help my mom.

"Dinner's on, boys," yells Dom a little while later. I hear the glass sliding door squeak shut.

When I get to the kitchen, Dom and Nick are already digging in. Nick reaches into the bag, grabs his food, and brushes past me down the hallway without a word.

"Sometimes he likes to be in his room by himself for a while. It's best to let him be," Dom says as he heads to his recliner. "Come grab a seat. Your mom's still out in the garage."

He nods to the other open recliner that's aimed at the TV. It's now playing some baseball game. He unfolds the foil wrapper of his burger on the tiny wooden stand next to him.

"I might go see how my mom's doing," I reply. "But thanks, though."

"Suit yourself," Dom says through a mouthful of food.

I wrestle with the sliding door and step back outside, the nighttime heat welcoming me back. At least I'm whale-come somewhere.

A Bestseller

With my disgusting mayo-and-mustard burger in one hand and a pouch of fries in the other, I go to the garage to find my mom sifting through her old belongings.

"By the way, you didn't have to keep Nick a secret." I look my mom right in the eye and her smile disappears. It's replaced with something that sort of looks like guilt.

She lets out a long sigh. "I'm sorry, G. I should've told you about Nick. I'd hoped it'd be a fun change of pace. Somebody your own age to hang out with. I know how hard it can be for you to make a real buddy. I didn't want you to be nervous."

"It's not that I can't make friends," I say as I near the mountain of junk. "It's that moving around all the time makes it feel kind of pointless." I sit down next to her and think back to all the friends I've said goodbye to over the last two years. I have a long list of people I never talk to anymore.

"Graham, I'm really sorry," Mom says again, cupping the back of my head with her hand in the way that always makes me feel like a little kid. "This is all so unfair to you."

I pull open the clear tape on one of the many boxes in front of us. "Find anything good?"

"Nothing of interest yet." She winks at me.

"How are you doing, G? I'm sure this has been a lot to take in today," Mom says, tiny beads of sweat forming on her slightly wrinkled forehead. "Nick okay?"

I shrug.

"I'm good. This place is cool. Sure, maybe it hasn't been *cleaned* in a couple years, but it's better than some hotel with little kids in wet swimsuits dripping all over the waffle station," I say, remembering the nights we've spent between housing situations.

Mom smiles at me kindly. She knows when I'm putting on a good face. "I'd hoped Dom had a spare room for you."

"I survived soccer camp last summer. This will be a breeze."

"That's my boy," Mom says.

"Never mind. I'm sure Nick's cool," I lie, looking around the garage. Piled in every corner are Harley motor parts, tools, and lots of Daytona 500 memorabilia.

"Think Dom's ever thought about selling any of this?" I wonder aloud. I take a few steps toward a wall covered in posters of fancy-looking boats. "Some of this stuff seems cool."

Mom doesn't say anything, and I look back to see her pop up from deep inside a cardboard-box mountain.

"What!" she says enthusiastically. "No way."

"No, I'm serious. The motorcycle stuff alone could get—"

"Oh, sorry, G. Not that. Wow . . ." she says, a mystified smile across her face.

"What is it?" I ask, hoping to find an unlocked safe or pirate treasure.

She pulls out a small, well-worn book instead. There isn't any cover art—I mean, there isn't even really a title or anything, so it's hard to tell exactly what it is. The pages are yellowed and worn like something you'd find in a museum.

"Wow. I can't believe it," Mom says, turning it over in her hands.

"Is it your diary or something?"

"*The Rare Birds of Florida*," Mom says, the leather journal slightly cracking as she opens it.

"Am I supposed to know that one?"

"A bestseller by Lindsay Dodds," she finishes.

"And again, I ask . . . what is it?"

"It's, oh I don't know . . . what me and Grandma Mabel used to do when I was young," Mom says. She turns it over in her hands. "One summer I was determined to find the ten rarest birds in Florida."

She passes it to me, and I open the cover to look at the first page. In sloppy cursive it reads *Property of Lindsay*. She crossed her *t*'s and swooped her *y*'s in the exact same way that I do.

"I found nine that summer. I never could find a Snail Kite."

"So, you've been a bird nerd your whole life then, huh?" I say. Mom smiles and I shut the book and try to hand it back over.

"Why don't you hang onto it for me, G," Mom says, reaching over to squeeze my hand. She returns to her pile of boxes as a gentle rain begins to fall outside.

"How does it feel to be home?" I ask her after a while.

"I'm not really sure I can even call this place my home anymore. Driving around tonight, it's all . . . different," she says, pulling out a high school yearbook and examining the cover. "Want to see a picture of your dad?"

I nod, a familiar lump in my throat. I try not to think about my dad too much, to be honest. I don't remember him really, so I don't know why thinking about him makes me feel sad.

She points to a picture of a guy who looks like a bizarro-version of me. He's older and taller, but still gangly like me. The lump in my throat bobs as I swallow. Seeing this picture reminds me that I've already lost one parent and could lose another. Before my cheeks get red, I blink a few times and look down. Mostly I don't think about the fact that my dad died. But when I *do* think about him, it feels like someone is squeezing my neck and my heart and my brain all at the same time.

"He was so handsome. Like you," she says, ruffling my hair. "Now, come on, let's head in. Before the bugs eat us alive."

THIS IS NEW

"Wakey, eggs and bakey," says a voice at the door of my—well, I guess Nick's—room. It's Dom, leaning in from the hallway. He's wearing a neon tank top that's covered in logos from a local surf shop. He has a ridiculous tan line on his arms from his T-shirts, like he's wearing a bright-white shirt under his tank. I should be wearing sunglasses as a precaution.

"Thanks, Dom," I say, wiping the sleep from the corners of my eyes. I can hear the sound of bacon crackling on a pan as the smell of it fills the air around me.

"Gettin' breakfast going. First day of practice for tryouts, got to be in fighting shape."

Nick groans as his dad heads back into the hallway.

"What are you practicing for?" I ask as I get up and make my bed. Maybe in a half-asleep state Nick won't be a total monster.

"Why do you care," Nick says glumly.

A monster at all hours, turns out.

Sometimes I remind myself that most people are good . . . and maybe are going through something tough. But right now, it's hard to do.

I hear Dom singing to himself in the kitchen, "Are you ready for some *foootballl*. And *hashbrooowwwnnnsss*."

I look around Nick's room and, besides the comforter, I don't really see anything a typical sports kid would have. There aren't any posters of people scoring touchdowns or empty Gatorade bottles lying around. Honestly, it all vaguely smells of fish.

"Football's cool. I tried it for about two weeks, but never really liked it. What position do you play?"

"Pretty much all of them," Nick responds.

"Wow that's intense," I reply. "You must be good."

Let the record show I am trying. Do you see that I'm trying?

"Yeah," he answers, finally getting up.

"I can help you practice later on, if you want," I say. Trying, like, SO hard.

"I usually work on my boat when I'm home," Nick says, stretching his arms over his head.

"Whoa, you've got a boat?"

"We found it. Out in the swamp. It barely works so I'm fixing it up," Nick says, grabbing his duffel bag for practice. "I've gotta go. I call dibs on the TV later."

"Yeah, I don't think I'll be around to watch anything, we—"

"See ya."

I set my jaw, ready to tell Nick that nobody wants to share his room, least of all me. That he doesn't have to be so rude. That he doesn't even know me at all.

Instead, I just watch him shuffle out of the room, the words sticking in my throat.

"There's my star linebacker," I hear Dom say over the clatter of cooking.

I tie the laces on my shoes and throw on a fresh shirt. For whatever reason I grab *The Rare Birds of Florida* before heading down to see what else breakfast, and today, will bring.

THE FLORIDA CLINIC

"OKAY. IT'S COMING UP NOW," MOM SAYS AS WE MAKE A LEFT TURN, following the road that's dotted with huge blue *H* signs.

We both look right, our eyes on the reason we're here: the Florida Clinic.

The hospital itself is huge and literally sparkling, sunbeams reflecting off the metal-and-glass structure. Mom turns off the radio, and we listen to the faint splashing of the giant water fountain that's outside of the hospital's main entrance.

I stare, wondering who's inside of it right now, what lives are being saved or lost at this exact minute. I wonder which families are pacing its hallways, hoping for a miracle of their own.

"You know what, G?" Mom says as we turn into the parking lot. "I think this might be the place."

And maybe it's the shimmering sunlight or the palm trees

clustered around the front entrance, but this hospital looks *different* from the other ones.

I look at my mom's expression. Her eyes are brimming with something that looks a lot like hope.

Maybe this one really *is* different.

Or maybe it's just the sunbeams.

THE SPECIAL DOORS

"HI THERE, ARE YOU MRS. DODDS?" ASKS A PEPPY MIDDLE-AGED WOMAN in lime green scrubs.

"I am," Mom replies, standing up to shake the woman's hand.

"Well, it's great to meet you. My name is LaDonna, and I'm going to be your coordinator for your time here," she says, her cheeks creasing with a bright smile. She nods my way. "I understand you have a son with you?"

"This is my Graham," Mom says.

"Pleased to meet you, Graham," LaDonna says, cracking a piece of gum between her front teeth with a wink. "I'm going to take your mom to do some grown-up stuff for a while. If you need anything at all, don't hesitate to ask."

I pause. I think about saying something. A joke, maybe, to keep the mood light. Something like, *well, for starters, my mom could use a heart that works. Do you have any in the back?* Instead, I just stay quiet.

"I hear they give out free chocolate chip cookies at the atrium coffee shop around this time," says LaDonna. "Perhaps that could be of interest to you?"

My eyes widen. "Yeah, maybe," I reply, even though I'm really excited by this news. My mom wiggles her eyebrows up and down at me. She knows my weakness for chocolate chip cookies.

I watch as the two head toward the special doors, the ones reserved for medical personnel only—the kind of doors not everybody gets to go through. There's no glass on them and they require a keycard to open.

Mom turns around as they are about to head inside. She's smiling, but I can tell it's the fake smile. The one she gives when she knows we're both too nervous to admit it. I give her the same fake smile back as the doors close.

Not everyone gets to go through the special doors. But my mom is not everyone. She is special.

THE GOOD ICE

AFTER HOPPING AN ELEVATOR OUT OF THE CARDIAC WING, I ENTER A brightly lit atrium on the first floor. There are a few shops on the perimeter of the circular room, including the gift shop, a fast-food taco place, and coffee shop. I step inside, under a wide dome of skylights, and see a smattering of tables and chairs filled with people clutching half-finished cups of coffee and tea. Some of them look like they've been up all night. A few look like they've been up all week.

"Excuse me, I was told there were free cookies?" I ask the man at the bakery counter.

"Yep. With any purchase. But that's not for another . . ." he says, looking at his watch. "Nineteen minutes."

I bob my head once in acknowledgement, weighing my options. Nineteen minutes to kill . . . and last week I may or may not have dropped my only gaming tablet in the toilet, so there's no chance I can zone out in a video game.

Thankfully, there's another important order of business that must be taken care of.

I head back toward the atrium. Cookies can wait.

If this were my first time in a hospital, I'd probably waste nineteen minutes by finding a magazine or watching TV nearby. But this is not my first time. I'm on a mission. One that involves finding the hospital's best-kept secrets.

In my expert opinion, a true hospital regular has to know at least a few things: any and all food establishments, the names of the nice nurses and janitors who will help you sneak around, and the location of the best ice maker.

This is harder than it sounds. Not all ice machines are created equal. Some give you the same old crushed stuff, and others dispense those little round pellets—but believe me, after a few years in and out of hospitals, you really start to get particular about things like different kinds of frozen water.

Back in the elevator, I lean against the railing and feel something stuffed into my back pocket—Mom's *Rare Birds of Florida*. I open the journal and mindlessly flip through the pages. I stop on an entry at random.

The Snail Kite

Characteristics: bird of prey, up to four-foot wingspan, some have blue-gray feathers, others are brown with streaks, bright orange beak and talons, eats apple snails (or as the French say, escargot!)

Habitat: Everglades, aka my backyard
Status: Endangered, thanks to humans
Sighting: Any day now, I can feel it!

"A bestseller," I mumble as the doors open on the second floor. Time to find some good ice.

Lou

After checking every ice machine on floors two through four, I have a solid contender in the orthopedic waiting room. As the elevator doors open on floor five, I know I must make it quick—it's only three minutes to cookie time.

I turn right and immediately see a standard tiny kitchen cove, around the corner from the pediatric waiting room. It's stocked with the normal stuff: fridge, sink, and microwave covered in the tiny splatters of reheated food—but in the corner is a big, shiny ice maker that looks brand new. So far, so good.

I grab one of the large paper cups from a dispenser near the sink and put it under the spout. The cup activates the motion sensor, and a glorious stream of frozen pellets spills into my cup. It smells like an ice rink, just after the Zamboni comes around. Absolutely incredible.

"Better be careful, that's the best ice in the whole joint. Don't want to waste it all."

I move my cup right before the ice avalanches onto the floor. I turn around, expecting to see some too-chummy doctor here to guzzle coffee.

Instead, it's a girl around my age. She's drinking water from a Florida Clinic–branded plastic mug, holding it with one hand and adjusting its long crinkly straw with the other. She has light-red hair that's pulled back and she's wearing a T-shirt with a technicolor butterfly on the front.

"You're new," she says. "I know everybody on this floor. You're definitely new."

"I am new. I'm Graham," I say, nervously. "Is *new* bad?"

"I'm Lou. Nice to meet you," she says, topping off her mug with water. "And *new* isn't bad at all. I like meeting new people."

She slams the cap back on her mug.

"And you're not seventy years old, so that's for sure new *and* different for around here."

"Yeah, my mom and I just got down here. She's waiting for a heart transplant," I say. "I'm not supposed to be up on this floor."

I tip back my cup of ice, letting it spill into my mouth. I crunch a few pellets. Wow. That is some good ice.

"Heart transplant?" she asks, raising her eyebrows.

"Yeah. Doctors all say Florida gives you a better chance."

"I hope you're right. We've been waiting for one, too. For my dad," she says. Lou hops up to sit on the light-gray countertop across from me.

Hospital kids are funny. Lots of them are used to talking about how they got here openly, like they're discussing the car they arrived in. And I'm totally not judging. I do it too.

"Oh. I'm sorry to hear that. Do you know where he is on the list?"

She shrugs. "Lately I've been doing my best to not think about it," she says. "Plus, I've figured out most everybody is going through their own stuff. It seems selfish to only be worried about myself."

I weirdly understand that feeling.

"What's that?" she asks, pointing to my mom's birding book.

"Oh, nothing really. My mom found this old journal of hers," I say, absentmindedly handing it over.

"And she let you read it?" says Lou, her eyes bright with wonder. "Aren't journals, like, private?"

"It's a birding journal," I clarify. "She started it when she was a kid."

"Did your mom grow up here?" Lou asks, flipping through the crinkled pages.

"Yup," I answer. "Do you live close?"

"Super close," Lou says, studying an entry about birds called Limpkins. I notice how she silently mouths the words as she reads along.

"So, are you here a lot then?"

"A few times a week," she says, shutting the journal and handing it back. "Just to keep an eye on my dad. Speaking of which, I should go."

Lou hops down to her feet and heads to the doorway leading into the hallway. She turns back my way.

"And if you need a nice janitor, look for Dorothy, Roxane, and Pedro. And Cheryl does weekends," she says, eerily simplifying my mission for the day. "It was nice to meet you."

"You, too," I reply. "See you around."

"See ya around, Graham," she says, darting back into the hallway and around the corner. She disappears almost as quickly as she appeared. I head the other way, back to the elevators and (hopefully) warm baked goods.

I decide I like Lou. She's weird, but good weird.

Kind of like me.

Days

Back in the atrium for round two, my stomach growls in anticipation for the cookies that will be coming my way. I order an iced tea from the bakery counter, and the barista gives me not one, but *three*, free cookies. I slide into a nearby booth with a smile.

For whatever reason I love sitting around in coffee shops like this. Why, you might be asking? I know what to expect. No surprises—well, sometimes there are if you order tuna salad, but you learn your lesson on that one the hard way, y'know?

I enjoy watching all the people that come to places like this. I try to imagine if they're feeling happy or sad. Sometimes I'll try and guess the names people are giving to the baristas to call out when the order is ready. I've learned that guessing names is tough, and that there are a lot more Carls and Rebeccas in the world than you'd think.

It gives me something to take my mind off whatever I'm think-ing, because I normally go to coffee shops during hospital visits with my mom. Especially on the Bad Days.

Bad Days are what me and my mom call the days we'd rather pretend never happened. When the news from doctors is the absolute worst. When she has to have yet another operation. When they still can't figure out how to help her. Those are the Bad Days. The kind where the only thing you can do is order an iced tea and watch the world go by.

The first Bad Day was in Chicago. We'd gone for a long day of tests and I had just sat down to lunch when my mom came in and sat in the booth across from me. I could see the worry all over her face. I knew something was very wrong. Even her eyes were frowning.

"Graham, I have to tell you something," she started. I'll save you the details, but this was the day we learned about her disease. The disease that makes her heart weaker with each passing day. The thing that has us chasing cures all over the country.

While my mom kept talking, I wasn't sure what to do or say, so I ate an entire flatbread pizza. Let's say it wasn't my finest moment. You take what you can get on the Bad Days.

But here, now, in this brand-new Florida Clinic? Well, some-thing feels different. I leave my booth and start walking back to the cardiac wing, extra treats in hand. I smile at the barista who gave me the cookies—a Carl, it turns out—and think, *heck, maybe, just maybe there are only Good Days ahead.*

SHAKE THERAPY

"THERE YOU ARE GRAHAM," SAYS A VOICE FROM BEHIND ME. I TURN AND see my mom and LaDonna come out into the lobby from the windowless doors. My mom is smiling for real this time.

I've been waiting for about fifteen minutes, gazing out at the slow-moving afternoon clouds outside the windows and eating more cookies than any supervised child would typically be allowed.

"You have a good day, Graham? I see you found the free cookies," says LaDonna, eyeing the crumpled paper bag next to me.

"It actually *was* a good day," I say, thinking of meeting Lou.

"Well, I'm feeling hopeful," Mom says. "How about you, Graham?" I can tell she's in a great mood, which means her appointment must have gone well.

"I guess I'm feeling the same," I answer, surprising even myself.

"Good. You know a day like this calls for one thing and one thing only: milkshakes."

"Mom, it's, like, ninety degrees out. And I can't imagine milkshakes are part of a heart-healthy diet."

"Then one extra-cold milkshake, just for you. I prefer stealing sips from yours anyways," she says, pulling the keys to the Blue Beast from her purse. She starts racing toward the elevators. "Last one to the van buys lunch!"

THE SNAIL KITE

"THIS LOT'S HOT!" SAYS A HUGE SIGN IN THE MIDDLE OF THE SWAMP behind Swansen's. We're staring at a billboard that has a photo of a real estate agent with teeth so white you could see them from space.

"They're trying to sell every possible inch of this state," Mom says, putting down the visor above the windshield to shield her eyes from the setting sun. "When I was little, Sugarland was as far west as anybody went. Now it seems like they're making a new city every few years. They'll start calling houses on stilts above a swamp 'waterfront' soon."

I finish chewing the last bite of my burger and start in on the remaining fries. *Waffle* fries. Incredible. I slurp at my milkshake. Perfection.

A breeze blows through and I try to roll my window down. Halfway down it gets stuck. The Blue Beast is full of surprises—like today I learned that the gas cap has to be bludgeoned shut and that just because a window can roll down, doesn't mean it will necessarily roll back up.

"Hey, y'all! Extra peanut-butter shakes and extra-crispy onion rings," says a chipper teenager in a bright-white polo shirt at my mom's window. The place is set up like an old school drive-thru, with servers running from car to car with trays of food.

"Oh, we already got our order," Mom calls out, as the server turns to run back to the kitchen.

"Oh really? Well, my ticket says it's for your spot and . . . my shift just ended," the server says back. "So, y'all have a good night!"

"Thank you so much!" Mom says. "We've got a couple of guys back home that will enjoy it all."

"Not before a few of those onion rings go missing, though." I grin.

"It all happens for a reason," she says with a knowing smile as she reaches for the largest of the fried rings.

Mom takes a bite but soon stops chewing. I follow her gaze and catch a glimpse of what looks to be the tail of a large bird as it disappears behind a tree about a hundred yards away. Through all the branches I see a quick flash of dark-gray feathers and bright-orange legs, but the bird is gone before we can fully see it.

"*Ohmhuhgyush?*" Mom says, her mouth full of food. She drops her onion ring. "*Dichoojuseadat?*"

"Did I see what?" I answer, fluent in Speakingwithyourmouthfull.

"Graham, I think *that* was a Snail Kite, entry number ten in *The Rare Birds of Florida,* by Lindsay Dodds."

"The bestseller?" I joke, taking a sip from my milkshake. It's almost too thick to pull through the straw.

"It's the only bird on the list that I've never seen. The rarest of them all."

I suddenly realize my mom is talking about *that* Snail Kite.

Mom unbuckles her seatbelt and removes the set of keys from the ignition. I look at the hospital band still around her wrist.

"Wait, what are you doing?"

"G, it's a sign. We have to find the Snail Kite. I just know that was it," she says, opening her door. "Get the journal. Let's go!"

The thrill of the chase surges through me.

I reach for my back pocket but—

Oh no.

It's . . . gone.

No Service

"Come on, G. Keep up!" Mom shouts from ahead.

"I'm comin'," I mutter, upset with myself for already losing one of my mom's prized possessions. Maybe it's just on the floor of the van. Or maybe I left it when I got those cookies?

When I catch up to Mom, she's huffing and puffing. Her eyes look wild. It's like she's possessed.

"They eat apple snails in marshes like this," Mom says as she cuts through a row of viny trees. The ground below us is squishy. "They usually fly together, too. We might see a whole family, Graham."

The terrain is starting to get wetter and wetter, with plants and trampled weeds giving way to bigger pools of muck. The kind that sucks your shoes off when you take too deep a step. I nearly trip as I catch a root on the ground below.

"You sure we should be out this far? Isn't this place full of stuff that's actively trying to kill us?"

"Everything's trying to kill you down here," Mom says dismissively, pushing her way deeper into the wilderness. "But it doesn't usually work."

Usually?

She's walking with a purpose, dodging any branches in her way. I look at the back of the real estate billboard we saw before. It's getting smaller as we put more distance between us and it. I look at my phone and watch one bar of reception drop to zero.

We come to the edge of a small bog, and I see a rustling high up in the branches of an oak tree. Leaves fall down like confetti, signaling something might be there. I start to get excited, thinking this might be the Whatever-Whatever bird my mom's so excited about. We might be witnesses to something cool and rare.

"Whoa, I think I see it!" I say as I spring forward.

My eyes are fixed on the tree above as I leave my mom behind, squishing over fallen branches.

"Mom, I think it's there!"

As I get closer, I swear I hear a bird, but I'm not sure exactly what I'm looking for.

"Mom, what does this thing look like? Should we do a call or something?"

I glance backward, but my mom's not close. She's back where I left her, leaning on a tree as she clutches her left shoulder.

I turn back, catching a glimpse of the bird as it flies behind a tree and out of sight. I look toward my mom again. She suddenly drops to her knees.

"Hey, are you okay?" I shout.

There's no reply.

"Mom!" I scream, my feet catching on the roots and mud as I run to her. "Mom!"

There's silence. An eerie and still silence.

Things seem like they're happening in slow motion. Like I can feel the weight of each step. My feet feel heavy and slow.

So.

Heavy.

So.

Slow.

"It's . . . I'm okay . . . I just . . ." she stammers, putting a hand on the ground. She tries to stand up but stumbles. She's trying to catch her breath but can't.

"I'm fine . . . just need a minute."

But if there's one thing I know, it's that she's definitely not fine.

BACK AT IT

I'M BACK IN MY WAITING ROOM AGAIN, ONLY THIS TIME THERE'S A STEADY beeping sound.

Beep. Beep.

The noises are coming through the off-white speakers scattered around the ceiling.

Beep. Beep.

Each one is starting to get louder and louder, with a few blips now coming in every so often. It's almost like Morse code—something my teacher in Buffalo made us learn.

Beep. Be-be-beep. Beep.

The sounds are getting so loud I put my fingers in my ears, trying to block it out.

Bfffpfpp. Bfffpfpp.

The sounds get even louder until it feels as if my eardrums might burst. Dust is falling down from the speakers as they rattle with extreme volume. The beeping gets faster and faster, and the only thing I can do is shout. Try to match it. Try and drown it out to beat its constant blaring. So I scream along.

"Aaaah!!! Aaaahhh!!!"

I yell louder and louder as the beeping speeds up, the rhythmic beats speeding up into a chaotic symphony.

"AAAHHH!!!"

And then I wake up and I'm staring at my mom in a hospital bed.

AWAKE

She's asleep, surrounded by noisy machines. An IV tube runs from her wrist to a clear bag hanging on a metal stand. Behind that is a row of steadily beeping machines and screens. It's always the same row of machines making the same sounds, whether you're in Seattle or Buffalo or everywhere else in between.

I watch the machine monitoring her heart rate, wishing I could do something. We've been here for hours and hours now. So long, I fell asleep. Back in the swamp, I didn't know what else to do so I started yelling *"Help, help, help! Somebody call 911!"*

"HELP!"

Just as I was losing hope, I heard the sirens. A minute later an EMT team burst through the trees and across the mud and all those gnarly roots.

They picked her up and got her in the ambulance, and the siren roared back to life. Once we got to the hospital, the doctors told me her defibrillator did its job. Technically. Most defibrillators shock a heart once, maybe twice, to snap it out of a dangerous rhythm. Hers did it more than *twenty* times.

But she was alive.

She is alive.

She. Is. Still. Alive.

HELLO, WAITING, MY OLD FRIEND

"Graham, honey, have you seen my phone?"

Mom's awake. My head hurts from sitting under fluorescent lights all day.

"Yeah, here it is," I say, finding it in a pocket of her purse and handing it to her. "Looks like you've got a few texts."

My mom's new home is on the third floor of the Cardiac Wing. They do all the tests and stuff on the first floor, but the real stuff happens the higher you go in a hospital.

The room is pretty much like any other hospital room—everything smells like latex gloves, including the food. At least this room has windows. I look out and see the parking lot light poles slowly flickering on, which means this Bad Day is finally coming to a close.

"Good, Dom is on his way over," she says, putting her phone on the rolling tray table positioned next to her bed. Her hair is pulled to one side, spilling over her blue hospital gown.

She opens the lid covering her dinner. "You hungry, babe?"

"What is it?"

"Grilled chicken," she replies, holding it up with her fork. "The grill lines may have been painted on, though, so who knows?"

"Yeah, I think I'm good on that." I fake a laugh. I don't have much of an appetite.

When the doctors came in a couple hours ago, they did the thing that doctors do, telling me I should stop by the nurses' station for a lollipop. Older people honestly still think lollipops are a thing, it's weird.

When I left, I stood right behind the door listening. They said she "has evolved to a level of care in which she needs to be consistently medicated and monitored," and blah blah blah.

It's all hospital jargon, meaning she can't leave the hospital and needs to be on liquid drugs and plugged into machines until they can get her a new heart.

"Well, you at least get my dessert," she says, tossing me a frozen cup of lemon-flavored sugar water. "I don't like the Italian ice."

I catch it and put it on the windowsill unopened. The condensation forms a ring on the cold metal. "Me neither."

"I'm sorry this isn't going the way we planned, G," Mom says, sipping a ginger ale.

"When have things ever gone the way we've planned?"

"I know. I just thought we'd have a little more time together before all . . . well, this," she says, gesturing to the monitors and medications.

"Hello? Anybody home?" comes a voice from the hallway.

Mom does her best to smooth her hair as Dom enters, wearing his signature paint-speckled white jeans and white shirt. He's not wearing sunglasses, which I figure is a sign of respect. The hospital lighting does his thinning hair zero favors.

"How ya doing, Linds?" Dom asks, giving her blankets an awkward pat. He places bottles of soda, juices, and energy drinks on her tray table. "I wasn't sure what you liked."

Energy drinks for the heart patient that can't have caffeine? The man is sweet but oblivious.

"Thank you so much, Dom," Mom says, lining up her drinks tallest to shortest. "We're doin' fine. It all happens for a reason."

"I want you to know Graham's in good hands, as far as that's concerned. I'll make sure he's taken care of."

Mom turns to me. Her eyes are tired. It's been a very long day.

Part of me feels bad leaving her in the hospital alone, but I know better than to complain about it. It's not as if I have another choice.

"Docs say anything about how this happened? I thought you were doing better?" Dom's tone is casual, but his leathered forehead is creased into deep valleys.

"Oh, you know . . ." My mom waves a tired hand.

"Looking for a bird. We went chasing after it behind Swansen's," I say.

"A bird! *Pfft.* Linds, you gotta be kidding me," says Dom.

"Not just any bird. A Snail Kite—there's a big difference," Mom says. Her eyes begin to have a tiny sparkle in them once again.

"Well, shoot. You better leave the chasing after birds to us from now on. At least to Graham here," Dom says definitively.

I nod for good measure. She looks at both of us and sinks back into her pillows.

"If we'd had five more minutes it'd have been worth it, too. I just know it was our bird," she says, closing her eyes with a grin.

A crew of nurses wearing green scrubs enters my mom's room for a shift change.

"Well, let's hit the road. We've got to get ready for tomorrow," Dom says. "Got a big job."

I walk over to the bed and give my mom a hug. She holds me tight and gives me a kiss on the cheek.

"See you soon, G."

"See you, Mom."

I follow Dom out into the hallway and we walk out to the van in silence. Dom seems to know when words only make things worse.

I like that about him.

TEN BUCKS AN HOUR

"WELL, WHATCHA THINK ABOUT SUGARLAND, KID?" DOM ASKS FROM THE driver's seat of his painting van. Besides the music from the radio, we've continued our silence in the car.

"Well, apart from nothing going according to plan, I really like it," I answer dryly.

"I know it must be tough. It's hard enough for me to see your mom like that. I can't imagine what that's like for you," Dom says, his face illuminated by the headlights of the car behind us.

Even though it's nighttime it's still warm out, and I can feel beads of sweat on the back of my legs.

A classic rock song comes to an end and the radio cuts to a commercial. Dom turns the volume down a bit.

"Dom, can I ask you a question?"

He turns the radio completely off.

"Fire away."

"Are me and my mom . . . in your way?" I ask, remembering what Nick said the day we arrived.

"Are you kidding me?" Dom says. "I'm upset you'd even think like that. I've known your mom basically my whole life. You're family as far as I'm concerned."

I don't say anything, but I can feel my shoulders relax a little.

"As a matter of fact, you should come work with me sometime," Dom continues. "I could use the help, and I'll give you ten bucks an hour. In no time you'll be a real Leo DaVinci."

From school I know that Leonardo da Vinci was a famous Renaissance painter. I imagine painting a mural of the Mona Lisa on one of the walls of My Waiting Room. I smirk at the thought.

As we come around a bend in the road, I see blurry red and blue lights in the distance. The cars ahead of us begin to slow as we approach the scene. My heartbeat picks up as we drive past.

"Oh man, it looks like a bad one," says Dom, whistling through his teeth.

Outside his window are police officers. They're trying to keep traffic moving, holding their left arms out and waving their right in circles. Behind them is an overturned SUV, the roof crushed in. The hood and all the windows are broken, and the passenger side looks completely mangled. Nobody's inside the car now, but there is an ambulance with its doors closed.

I know that somebody is inside there right now. And from the looks of it, it might be bad.

"Send 'em good thoughts, Graham," Dom says. "About all we can do right now."

Good thoughts. That their Bad Day won't turn into a Very Bad

Day. My heartbeat picks up as we drive. I wish very hard that whoever is in that car will be okay.

And . . .

Also . . .

There is something else.

I hate this thought before I even have it, but I'm realizing that if my mom gets a heart, a new heart, it won't exactly be *new,* you know? You only get a Good Day because someone else, and their family, is having the ultimate Bad Day. It's different than a kidney, where you somehow get two and can just, like, share. You can't live without a heart. And you can't give someone a heart and live. Something tragic has to happen, like an accident.

As we leave the wreck behind, my throat gets tight. All this time, I've been hoping, praying, and counting down the days for my mom's new miracle heart . . . for my mom to live . . . but suddenly I can't stand the thought. My stomach turns sour.

I'm not sure if it's what we just witnessed, or heading back to an awful roommate, or remembering that I lost my mom's prized bird journal in only a day, but I feel like crying.

Dom clears his throat.

"It's all reasoning to happen," he says, doing his best to try and remember my mom's famous saying. "Er, wait."

And despite the somber mood, we both chuckle.

"Something like that," I say as I wipe away the tears that have found their way to my cheeks. Dom keeps the radio off for the rest of the way home, nothing but the buzz of insects and the rattle of the van as our soundtrack.

A TRUCE

I WAKE UP TO THE CLANGING OF POTS AND PANS IN THE KITCHEN.

"*Buenos días*," says a deep voice. "I'm Carlos. If you want any *café*, help yourself."

My eyes adjust to the bright light of the kitchen as I begin to smell doughnuts and coffee. I just couldn't deal with Nick last night, so I slept on one of the leather recliners in the living room. I yawn, my neck sore from sleeping on two different chairs in a twenty-four-hour period.

According to the dusty clock in the kitchen, it's just after nine. I realize I slept in, and the painting crew is arriving now. I'm still in the same clothes from yesterday.

I groan and get up, half-asleep. I see a light on in the bedroom and walk toward it, my footsteps silent on the shag carpeting.

"What do you want?" Nick says as I enter the doorway. He's

awake and holding a piece of rope that he's using to practice tying different knots.

"I might paint with your dad today. Do you have any extra of those Dom and Son shirts?" I say as I sit on my bed, massaging my tense neck muscles. "All my stuff is dirty."

"Make him give you one," Nick says, making a point not to look at me. "Why should I have to?"

"Shouldn't you be working for him anyway?" I ask.

"Says who?" Nick says, shooting me a glare.

I point at the logo literally right under his nose. "Um, the shirt?"

"Dad doesn't care. The last thing he needs is me working for him," Nick says, kicking the circular knot he just lassoed.

"Why do you say that?"

"I just can't," Nick says, annoyance creeping in his voice.

"I'm sure if you asked him, he'd let you—"

"I'm color-blind, okay? I messed up a big room once, and he's never let me come back." His eyes are pinned to the rope. He leans forward, slouching like a half-deflated balloon animal.

"Oh," I say. We're silent for a moment. *Now who's the mean one?*

"Is your mom doing okay?" Nick asks, looking up at me. His voice is suddenly quieter. He looks . . . worried.

I pause, unsure if Nick just had a personality transplant in front of my eyes.

"She will be. I think," I say. "Thanks for asking."

"I don't know what I'd do if my mom died," Nick says, suddenly very serious.

"Yeah," I say, because, what else is there really to say?

"I thought it'd be funny, sending you the onion rings and peanut butter shakes. Have you ever heard of a grosser combo? But anyway, then I watched you and your mom chase that bird and then I heard you calling for help . . ."

My brain tries to catch up to what he's saying. "Wow . . . wait. You were at Swansen's? So *you* were the one who called?"

Did he seriously save my mom's life?

Nick clears his throat as if he's about to say something but then the doorbell rings.

"Who's using the front door?" Nick asks in a tone that means *nobody ever does that*. He walks into the hallway and through the kitchen.

"And where is your mom? Does she live close?" I ask, following him. I'm realizing I've never heard him talk about her.

"Here's your answer: yeah, I called. Maybe I was hoping the ambulance would take you with it, too—out of my room and out of my life," Nick says as he stomps to the door.

I clench my teeth. "Well, um, I owe you one," I say awkwardly, following after him as the bell rings again, this time three rings in a row. Before I turn the corner to the front door, I hear Nick open it up.

"Who are you?" he says gruffly.

"Does Graham live here?" says the voice.

I come around the corner and see someone standing on the tattered welcome mat. It's Lou, from the hospital. She's wearing one of those white captain hats, the kind with a stitched-on anchor and tiny gold rope.

"Hey! Graham!" she says, her eyes lighting up.

The day is already hot and balmy, and I can feel the sticky humidity quickly creeping into the air-conditioned house.

"Do you two know each other?" Nick asks, crossing his arms.

"Yeah. Hey?" I say to Lou with a small wave.

"I think you lost something," Lou says. She opens her tan corduroy backpack and reaches inside. She pulls out *The Rare Birds of Florida,* by Lindsay Dodds.

"Lou! You are the best person alive!" I shout. "You just saved my life. Seriously. Where was it?"

"Ice maker."

Of course. I refilled after the coffee shop. I reach out to take back the missing book, but Lou tucks it behind her back.

"Um?" I ask, still holding out my hand.

"I'm going to give this back to you, but on one condition," she says.

"Wait, how did you figure out I live here?" I ask, realizing how weird this is. I look out at the front lawn and see a bicycle strewn sideways.

Lou shrugs. "I have my ways."

I give her a look that means *but seriously though.*

"Fine. Nurse's station," Lou says with a smirk.

"Wait. I've seen you before. You live a few streets over," Nick says with a skeptical look.

"I do," Lou replies.

"Then how come I've never seen you in school?"

"I do homeschool," she says. "But back to what I was saying, *Graham,* I noticed that your mom never found the Florida Snail Kite,

64

which is, like, super rare in Florida. And the reason that's important," she pulls out a folded piece of paper, "is *this*."

Lou opens it and my eyes immediately are drawn to the top, which reads: *$5,000 PRIZE.*

"Someone's giving away five thousand bucks?" Nick asks, leaning in to take a look for himself. Lou hands him the contest flyer.

"Not someone, the Florida Birding Society," Lou explains. "The Snail Kite is struggling to survive in Florida, so they're raising awareness for it. Only kids thirteen and under can enter. The first person to snap a photo of themselves and the bird gets the cash."

"That's a lot of money," Nick says, his eyes shining. "I could fix up my boat with that."

"We could fix up a lot of boats with that, Huck Finn," Lou says. "But take into account that we'll be splitting it evenly."

"I'm Lou, by the way," she says, offering Nick her hand.

"Nick," he says, shaking hands with a fake tough-guy voice. He hands the printout back to Lou and she passes it to me. "You know they make apps and stuff to find birds, though."

"And that's exactly why this is exciting: apps are allowed, you just have to be a kid. It's in the rules, something about trying to get us outdoors," Lou answers. I begin to study the fine print of the contest, but Lou snatches it back from my hand.

"I think we should do it," she says. She looks so excited that her heels are bouncing a little on the pavement. "I mean, what are the odds that your mom knows where to find a rare bird worth a bucket of cash? It's like fate."

"Wait, how did you find out about this contest?" I ask.

"Have you ever heard of Google?" she asks.

I roll my eyes. "Yeah, but like how—"

Lou cuts me off by tossing the journal at me. As I grab it, I remember the way my mom's eyes lit up as she talked about finding this bird. Lou looks almost the same. Maybe this *is* fate or something.

"After reading your mom's journal, I did some research about birds. And boom. It was, like, the first thing that popped up," Lou continues.

"That flyer says the contest ends next Saturday at midnight, a week from tomorrow. You do realize that we might not win the contest, even if we find it somebody else might beat us to it." I hedge.

"True, but if we *do* find it, we'll finish your mom's journal for her."

She has a point. Besides, I like the idea of doing something nice for my mom, with or without the money. Maybe painting with Dom can wait for another day.

"If we work together, I bet we could find it. Maybe even in the swamp you guys call a backyard."

"That's my swamp," says Nick. "And I know every inch of it. I've seen all kinds of birds back there."

"The contest website suggests having a camera with a zoom lens, some binoculars, and a comprehensive birding guide," Lou says. "I found exactly none of those things, but brought my phone and this."

She pulls out a large magnifying glass that seems old enough to have discovered the first dinosaur bones. She holds her phone's camera lens up to it.

"Good enough for our first mission! Well, what are we waiting for?" Lou says. "Let's go!"

"Nick, can your boat fit three people?" I ask, turning to him. This feels important and exciting.

"It could," he says hesitantly.

"What, are you scared?" Lou asks.

Nick makes a face. "I'll show you scared," Nick says. "There's probably a bird guide and some life jackets in the garage. Better go grab 'em, unless you wanna fall overboard and give me your cut of the prize money."

Lou sprints into the garage through its open door. Nick and I are standing alone in the entryway to the house.

"Thanks again, man," I say to Nick. "With my mom."

"Whatever. You owe me," he answers, back to his old self. "Now let's go get some weird bird money."

THE BABY BLUE BEAST

GASOLINE IS A LOT LIKE GLITTER, I'M REALIZING. LIKE, IF YOU DO A craft with glitter on a Monday, on Thursday you are still finding little shiny dots on your eyelid/ear/toothbrush. I say this because right now I'm carrying a tiny red container filled with fuel for Nick's boat, and I'm pretty sure I'm going to smell like a chainsaw for a week.

"Heads up," Nick says. He's ahead of me and Lou by about five feet. Nick lets go of something and I duck under a leaf-filled branch that almost whacks me in the face. We've been walking on a path for about five minutes now, and each step is feeling less pathlike and more swamplike.

It's really cool, though. The trees above us are gnarly and twisty, almost like we're in a creepy fairy tale. Slightly different from Buffalo, I'd say.

"Does your boat have a name?" asks Lou, her arms still filled with the three life jackets. Nick's carrying an oar and a tiny anchor attached to fraying yellow rope.

"*The Baby Blue Beast.* Like my dad's crummy van," Nick answers softly. "I think it's boring, but technically he's the one who found it during a painting job on the canal, so he said he had naming rights."

The trail comes to a *T* and we follow Nick as he hangs a right.

"What would you call it, if you could change it?" Lou says.

"Hm. I don't really know. Guess it never crossed my mind since it wasn't really an option," Nick replies. After a moment he adds, "Maybe the SS *Suzanna*."

"Who's that?" I ask.

"My mom," Nick says, a twig loudly snapping under his weight.

"Where's she?" says Lou. "Judging by the fact you guys still had Halloween decorations up, I figure she doesn't live at that house."

I raise my eyebrows, wondering if Lou will get the same response I did.

"You sure do ask a lot of questions," Nick mumbles.

"Correct," she replies.

"Whatever. Where my mom lives isn't important."

"If we're going to be business partners, we've got to be honest with—" Lou continues.

"Whoa! Everybody freeze," Nick hisses. He's frozen, staring at the muddy ground in front of him. I stand completely still.

"What is it?" I say, starting to sweat. It feels like it's getting hotter with each passing second.

Nick stoops down to study the trail.

"Probably possum tracks. For a second, I thought it might be something, ah, bigger," Nick says as he stands up and continues down the path.

Um, *probably?* While I'm not versed on the specifics, I'm pretty sure Florida has a lot of poisonous creatures that would be eager to feast on us. Not to mention, gators.

"So, homeschool, huh. How is that? I thought it was only for people that are weird," Nick says to Lou.

"Homeschool is the best," Lou says. "I can do school whenever I want, and I'm never stuck inside a classroom."

That does sound intriguing. Plus, your class can't be filled with jerks and bullies if your classmates are your pets and LEGOs.

"Whatever. Still sounds weird to me," Nick answers. "Boat's coming up soon."

We duck under a few more tree branches and soon see a small inlet of water and a dock that's about ten feet long, its wooden slats shiny with a new coat of stain. At the end of it, tied up with a thick rope, is a blue boat. It looks like a big bathtub with bench seats. The paint is peeling off from sun exposure.

I hand Nick the gas container, and he connects it to a clear tube that runs to a trolling motor in the front of the boat. It's small, with a tiny propeller no bigger than a dinner plate.

"All aboard."

Lou hops on without hesitation, grabbing a seat in the back. She's holding the closest thing we could find to a bird guide in the garage, something called *Tony Mangione Explains Hawks*. It seems crinkled from water damage, so we'll see if it's any help.

I climb into the middle of the boat, brushing away a couple of cobwebs near my feet. My only boat experience comes from watching reality TV shows about yachts in hospital waiting rooms, so I'm unsure how to tell if Nick's boat is seaworthy.

"This thing will work with all three of us?" I ask.

"Only one way to find out," Nick says as he hops in the front. He presses a latch and tilts the motor, dipping the propeller blades into the greenish water. He grabs the plastic handle on the rope-start and pulls hard, like starting a lawnmower.

Burburbuburbuburburb.

The tiny motor comes to life as Nick takes his seat just behind it. He grabs the steering handle and gives it the gas. We slowly start to move. And even though we're only going four, possibly five miles per hour, I have to admit that this is kind of fun.

On either side of us are banks covered in vines and long grass. Every now and then a frog or turtle slips away from its hiding spot as we go past. The air over the water smells gross, like taking a whiff of rotten eggs. Soon, the channel of water gets bigger. At the dock it was maybe seven or eight feet across, but now that's almost doubled. Sun is filtering through the tree line above us. It's peaceful out here. I smile and look back at Lou. She's smiling too.

Screech. Screeeeech.

Somewhere in the dense swamp we can hear the call of a bird.

"That the one we want? All the pictures in this birding guide look like those drawings of turkeys you make using your hand," Lou asks, shielding her eyes as she looks in the book, then toward the area of the bird call.

"I don't think so. That sounded like—"

"A crow, I'd say," Nick interjects. "They eat the roadkill from the highway that's just over that way."

"That's where we are? I live near there." Lou scans the channel. "That's awesome. I wonder how far you could get if you kept going in this direction."

"All the way to the other side of Sugarland, going east," Nick says, turning back toward Lou. "If you had enough gas, these canals could take you the whole way to the ocean. But my dad says it's nothing but everglades and trouble past the third bridge that's up ahead."

The trees are thinning out and the small channel is opening up into a bigger body of water. The sides of it are filled with lily pads and swamp grass.

And while it's the hottest part of the day, when most animals are hiding from the sun, to my left I see a Great Blue Heron standing in the water, its long and slender legs stepping through the muck. I stealthily pull out my phone and snap a photo of it, grinning, and I look back at Lou again to make sure she's seen it, too.

But she's not even looking up. And her lively eyes are gone.

"Oh," she says, looking down at her phone.

"What is it?" I ask.

Nick eases off the gas and the boat idles, thick weeds and marshland on either side of us.

"Nothing. It's fine," she says, but she's still nervously tapping her phone with her fingernails.

"Doesn't seem like nothing," I say gently.

"It's just I don't have service out here, that's all. And my dad's got stuff going on. He might need me," she says. I can hear the worry in her voice.

"You want to head back?" I ask.

"No way," Nick says. "We haven't found the bird yet." But before Nick can say anything else, we all turn our heads toward another sound.

Splash!

The end of a scaly tail flicks back and forth quickly before it disappears below the surface of the water. My pulse begins to race.

"Whoa!" Nick exclaims. "Now *that* was an alligator!"

"No way," Lou says, perking up in her seat.

"Seriously? A gator? Can those things jump in here?" I ask, surveying just how tall the sides of the boat are. I keep looking at the water but all that's left is a trail of bubbles and a sense of total fear.

"Let's not find out," Nick says, revving the engine and turning us back around. I keep my eyes fixed on the area of the gator, but there's nothing else. I'm beginning to panic, sweat forming at the sides of my head. The water is so dark and murky it's impossible to see whatever is lurking below.

As my gaze stays on the last of the rising bubbles in the water, though, I see a familiar reflection. It's a bird. A big one. And honestly—though I can't be sure—I think it's similar to the bird Mom saw at Swansen's. Maybe it's even the same one.

I look up in the sky but can only make out tail feathers disappearing into an outcropping of trees.

"Wait! Stop!" I shout, but Nick continues on.

"Are you crazy, man? We're not stopping with that thing around," he says.

I stand up in the boat, wobbly and unstable. My panic is somehow gone.

"I swear that was a Snail Kite," I say, peering in the direction where it flew. "What are the chances of that?"

As Nick guides us home, I keep my eyes fixed on the sky, scanning to see if the bird might make another pass. It never does.

Somehow, though, I get the feeling that I can do this; I can find this bird, win the money, and finish what my mom started.

I close my eyes for a second, the hot wind in my face, and it's like I'm in My Waiting Room once again. But all of a sudden, there's something new. A small window, where I can stand on my tiptoes and look out with hopes of seeing a bird in the distance. And I know it's only a tiny sliver of a window, but it's got to be a sign that the Snail Kite is begging me to come find it.

I open my eyes, more certain than ever that I'm supposed to be on this journey. Maybe, in some weird way, it might even help my mom. I imagine the joyful look on her face when I tell her that we found the bird and I completed her journal.

"Graham, you coming?" Lou asks, climbing back on the dock.

I take one last look back at the water, which is shimmering with sunbeams cast through the trees.

"It all happens for a reason," I say under my breath .

"What?" Lou yells, already heading back down the path.

"Nothing," I call back, certain that my journey to find this rare bird has only begun.

TIME TO GET SERIOUS

"I CAN'T BELIEVE WE ALMOST FOUND THAT BIRD ON THE FIRST DAY OF looking," I say to Nick from across the room. "What are the chances?"

"Right," Nick says as he climbs into his bed. "You do know there's a ton of birds that look exactly like the one you're after, yeah?"

He reaches and turns off the light on his nightstand.

I'm looking up at the ceiling. There's a few of those glow-in-the-dark stars and planets that are stuck up there, but their green glow seems faded and tired.

Ding!

From the floor's shaggy carpet my phone lights up with a text. I squint and look at the screen. It's from Lou, to both me and Nick:

> Tomorrow. Same time. Same place. But with real binoculars, a working camera, and a birding guide that has actual photos of birds. Time to get serious.

"There's a text from Lou," I say, yawning as I type back that I'll be ready. "Looks like we're back at it tomorrow."

Nick doesn't answer, but after a few seconds turns the light back on.

"So now I have to take you guys out whenever you want? Like I'm your tour guide or something?"

"Oh. No, I guess I just thought we were partners—"

"Whatever," he says.

There's a pause where neither of us say anything, and I can hear the faint sounds of big, fat raindrops hitting the roof of the house. I watch as Nick picks up his phone and types out a message, but nothing comes in the thread with me and Lou.

"Just meet me in the garage at ten tomorrow morning," he says as he turns off the light once again.

A WINDOW

I PUT MY PHONE DOWN AND CLOSE MY EYES.

Instantly, I'm in My Waiting Room. I can tell it's early morning.

The little window is back, giving me a peek of the outside world. I stand up and walk over to it, trying to peer outside, but it's like staring straight at a spotlight. I shield my eyes with my hand and take a step backward.

The ray of sunshine stretches and shifts over the gross tan carpeting. It begins to creep from the floor to a chair and finally closer and closer to one of the doors in My Waiting Room—the one that leads to my mom getting her transplant. To all of this being behind us.

I open my eyes and smile in the darkness. If—no, *when*—I find this bird, I just know everything will be different.

It has to be.

BIRD FACTS

"HOLD ON. SAY THAT AGAIN FOR ME. IT'S A WHAT?" I ASK LOU, WHO IS standing in the garage next to the mountain of my mom's old stuff. She's wearing a tan bucket hat with a matching vest. There's what looks to be a fishing hook with fake yellow feathers stuck to her new choice of headwear. In her hands is an open book with various birds printed all over it.

"It's a parliament. You know how, like, a group of crows is called a *murder*?" Lou says, flipping to a page in her new birding book. "It says that birders are serious about naming groups correctly. So, a group of owls is a parliament. A flamboyance is a huge amount of flamingos. There's lots more."

"This seems like a lot to remember," I say, leaning in close to try to read for myself. "Where'd you find this book?"

"The library. It's one of my favorite places," Lou says, flipping through pages.

"I saw another poster for the contest there, too. Tons of kids were looking at it. We've got competition and no time to waste. The contest ends in a week." I watch as Dom's tiny cat runs across the driveway. It's humid, and the sun is almost finished soaking up the small pools of rainwater that formed there last night.

"I also found this camera. My dad said he never uses it anymore, and it's got a zoom lens and everything. The only thing left to find is a pair of binoculars," Lou says, tucking her book under one arm as she hands over a bulky black-and-silver camera. I hold it up to my eye, zooming in on a puddle in the driveway.

I can feel my T-shirt starting to cling to my underarms, and I have to squint because the sun is already peeking above the trees. *Where is Nick?*

"I just feel like I want to know *everything* there is to know about birds now. Don't you?" Lou asks.

"Oh," I mumble. "I guess."

"You *guess*?" she replies, her face crinkling. "We're not going to find this bird and win that cash with 'you guess.' No, we have to be serious. Hold on."

Lou turns to a chapter and holds a finger to the page. There's a small picture of the Snail Kite in the center.

"See? This is what I mean. We need to know our stuff. Bird facts," she says, clearing her throat. "Bird fact: young Snail Kites take at least two weeks to use their beaks to eat snails from their shells."

"Are we sure this is all true?" I ask. "On that other page it said that a group of chickadees is called a *banditry*, which one hundred percent has got to be made up."

"If it's in here, it's a verifiable bird fact."

I chuckle.

"Then maybe I'll make my own list," I offer.

"Yeah? *The Graham Guide to Birds*?" Lou jokes.

"I must admit, it has a certain ring to it. *The Graham Guide to Birds*," I say, spreading my hands, like it's an invisible banner above us. "Bird fact number one is: a goose is actually an angry duck."

Lou laughs loudly. It's surprising and quick and sort of sounds like the cackle of someone's aunt.

"Well, at least you're getting into it now," Lou says as she continues to look in her library book. "What else do you like to do, other than lie about animals?"

"Like hobbies?"

"Sure. I'll go first, even. Last year I got really into botany. Spores, trees, everything. At one point I owned eleven ferns, which I learned is way too many ferns," Lou says. "I'm pretty good at making friendship bracelets, too, like this one."

She holds out her left wrist and on it is an orange bracelet, its twisted strands adorned with a few multicolored beads.

"I can make you one sometime," Lou says. "That's the only problem with homeschool, I guess. Tons of bracelets, but not too many people to give them to."

"The only thing I'm good at making are these tiny origami animals," I answer. "My rabbits are pretty good, so are my butterflies. When I'm just sitting somewhere I kind of need something to do to keep myself busy, you know?"

"I definitely do," Lou replies.

"I usually try and hide them in places for people to find. Like a little secret," I continue. "When you had that shirt with a butterfly on it the other day it gave me the idea to leave a few around the hospital."

Lou doesn't look up, still studying her book intently, but reaches into her pocket and pulls out a light-green butterfly. She looks up with a bright smile, then pushes the tiny paper animal back into her pocket for safekeeping. I search for something to say, but I don't know what it would be.

"Wait a minute," Lou says, pulling the book close to her nose. "It says that the best time of day to find a Snail Kite is sunrise or sunset."

I look at my phone and see it's now 10:27.

"Where's Nick?" Lou says, slamming her book shut. "It's way past sunrise, and we're sitting here like a bunch of suckers. Didn't he get my message?"

"He's the one who said to meet in the garage. And he's the one who was gone when I woke up."

"Let's get to the dock," Lou says. "Maybe he's already getting the boat ready for us to go out."

Lou puts her book and camera back in her bag and starts toward the same path we took to Nick's dock, following the muddy imprints of shoes from yesterday. I'm surprised they still look fresh.

"Can you hear that?" Lou says. I'm following, doing my best to dodge the same branches and tree limbs.

"Hear what?" I pause. The chirping of the birds begins to settle, and I finally hear what she's talking about.

Burburburb.

It's the unmistakable gurgle of the tiny motor . . . on Nick's boat.

"He must've set it up and everything," Lou says, hurrying her walking pace.

I follow after her, finally reaching the clearing that leads to the dock. But as we get closer, I get an uneasy feeling when I see that the boat is already out in the water.

And I see two other kids already on it.

"Tweet-tweet, bird nerds! Who's going to win now?"

SOUTHERN HOSPITALITY

"HEY! TRAITOR!" LOU HOLLERS AS WE TAKE OUR FIRST STEPS ONTO THE wooden dock. "We were partners!"

Nick and his boat are twenty yards away. One of the kids is taller and stockier than Nick, and the other is tiny and wiry. They both are wearing bright white Florida State hats over their curly dark brown hair and clothes that are way too fancy for a swamp. Their khaki shorts are clean and look freshly ironed. They both have on bright blue and orange polo shirts.

"These the two you were telling us about?" says the tallest one, cracking a blue piece of gum in his mouth. "The out-of-towner and the weirdo?"

"Nice clothes. Do you work at a zoo?" the shorter one sneers at us. He takes a seat on the boat.

Lou walks to the end of the dock, the wooden slats creaking underneath her every step. I follow behind, watching as long-legged spiders tiptoe over the water's surface.

"*We* were supposed to go out today," Lou yells at Nick.

"Says who?" Nick shouts back. "I didn't say that."

He turns the motor off, and his boat slowly begins to drift in the swampy water. The banks of this small inlet are filled with tiny, croaking frogs. As Nick's boat gets closer, they take turns darting, swimming, and jumping away.

"We heard about your contest," says the boy sitting down. He's wearing shiny aviator sunglasses. "Five grand? That seems like a prize that should go to somebody who deserves it."

"Who *are* you guys?" Lou says.

"Right, where's our southern hospitality?" the kid asks sarcastically. "We're Nick's *real* friends. I'm DJ and this is my older brother Zane. We're Nick's partners to finding this stupid Swamp Sparrow or whatever."

"You don't even know what it is!" Lou replies, frustrated. "Actually, no, maybe that's a good thing. There's no way you're finding a real rare bird by Saturday. I guarantee it."

The taller one snorts a laugh and chomps his gum before spitting into the water, introducing a mixture of saliva and cool mint flavor crystals into the ecosystem.

"Yeah, why do you guys even care about this contest?" I ask.

"'Cause this is our swamp is why I care. Who said we needed y'all here?" asks DJ. "And the contest will be over as of next weekend. We're coming back with our dad's boat to win it. It's super nice. Way better than this piece of junk."

I look at Nick, who doesn't react, even though his friend just bad-mouthed his beloved craft. I'm surprised since it seemed like he was really proud of that thing.

"You guys take your stupid boats, we don't need one anyways," Lou says.

I don't say anything, even though I'm pretty sure we *do* need Nick's boat if we want any chance of finding a Snail Kite. The idea of these guys out on the water, having the time of their lives and finding *my mom's* bird makes me angry—really angry. I force myself to unclench my fists. I don't want them to know I'm mad. I know from experience that that usually makes things worse.

"Let's go back to our house, Nick. Our mom is gone on a lunch thing or whatever," says DJ.

Nick pulls on the ripcord to the motor and it starts back up. The boat starts to leave the dock with a trail of tiny bubbles behind it.

"See you around," he says. I keep looking him in the eye, but he won't meet my gaze.

As the boat motors away the bigger kid stoops down and picks up a strand of seaweed. He throws it toward us, missing us, but splashing the water in front of the dock. Nick's two friends laugh. As we walk off the creaking dock, I watch as Lou turns back.

"He totally ditched us," she mumbles.

"Yeah," I agree. Even though nothing really happened, my heart won't stop racing and I'm not quite sure why.

THE LIST

WE DON'T SAY ANYTHING FOR ABOUT A MINUTE AS WE WALK BACK TOWARD Dom's house, but then Lou stops in the middle of the path. She's looking up at the canopy of trees above us. A few sunbeams are making their way through the cover of leaves overhead. It feels like the lighting when you're in a sudsy car wash, you know? When it's not bright, and not dark, and all the shades of light keep shifting.

"How's everything going with the transplant? Where are you guys on the list?" Lou asks, brushing her hair behind her ears. After how excited she was earlier, I can tell her mood has changed. She seems sad.

"They say she's way up the list," I reply. "But you never really know, I don't think."

Getting to the top of the list is a big deal for anyone waiting for a transplant. It's like getting an invitation to the most private and exclusive party that ever existed.

Some people, if they're really sick, don't wait on the list for very long. Sometimes, though, people wait years and years and nothing ever happens.

There are a lot of factors but it seems like you need to be in the right place at the right time. My mom is now "dual-listed," which means she's on the waiting list in Buffalo *and* down here, too. Her hometown hospital, The Florida Clinic, actually has the shortest wait-list for heart transplants of anywhere we've looked. It's the reason we came down here, really. For a better chance.

"Your mom must be really strong," Lou says. "Being stuck in the hospital all day like that."

I think about my mom, trapped in her room, like a hostage to her own heartbeat. I think about her all the time, wondering if she's okay, if she's happy and smiling. Or if at this very moment the machine in her chest is shocking her heart to keep it beating, or if a team of doctors is rushing in to save her. I can see the look on her face in the hospital bed—just like it was in the swamp, totally unresponsive.

"You alright?" Lou asks.

I exhale. "Yeah. Some days it all seems like a bad dream, huh?" Usually, I have to explain myself to other kids, but not to Lou. She gets it. She's going through it with her dad.

Lou nods. "But even bad dreams have to end, Graham Dodds," she says knowingly, as she starts to walk again. I try to stay next to her, matching her hiking pace. "And now, we have to figure out how to find our bird without a boat."

"You have any ideas?"

"I'm working on it." She grabs her phone and glances at it as we leave the trail and get to the green grass of the backyard. The ground is spongy underneath us, and it smells as if the yard was freshly mowed.

"How's your family doing?" I ask her. I realize in the few times we've talked I've never heard Lou talk much about her dad's situation.

"Oh, about the same. Ups and downs," Lou murmurs. She looks at her phone again. Her face goes sullen. "I should head to the hospital anyways. We have a lot of tests and stuff coming up in the next few days."

We get to the garage and Lou takes off her new hat, her face missing the excitement it had before. She stuffs her new outfit into her backpack, jamming it next to the giant birding book.

"I'll go with you," I say. "I should probably go see my mom."

"It's okay. I think I'll go by myself," she says. "See you around, Graham."

"Sounds good."

Lou hops on her bike and heads off, the last of the rain puddles soaked up by the vibrant sun.

OFFICIAL

As I finish brushing my teeth before bed, I hear my phone buzz with a text. I walk over and see a photo from Lou. It's her hand holding a half-finished friendship bracelet, a bunch of loose orange-and-yellow strands beginning to form one uniform band.

> You're getting a bracelet. It's official: we're friends.

I look closer and can see the background is the print the Florida Clinic uses for their bedsheets. Looks like Lou's killing time, finding something to do while spending a long night at the hospital with her dad. I message her back:

> It's settled. Friends.

WHO'S WHO

IT'S SUNDAY MORNING, AND SINCE NICK WAS GONE WHEN I GOT UP, I'VE been able to get ready in peace. I know he's probably off hunting for the prize money with his friends, but at least it's quiet.

The sun is high enough in the sky to be in my eyes, and I'm filling my backpack full of stuff I figure I'll need to survive my long day of sitting around in a hospital.

Usually my list is the same: a phone charger, for obvious reasons. A water bottle, for preserving the best ice samples. A hoodie, because every hospital is roughly 58 degrees inside. And last, but not least, candy. I always try to hide as many pieces in as many different pockets as possible. Oh, and typically a gaming device, if it's not ruined by toilet water.

I was searching around the garage last night, though, and found an old battery-powered dice game with no batteries, so maybe I can locate some and make it work. I also found a book about drawing and calligraphy to bring along, too. I'm not sure who it belongs to, but figure it'll give me something to do for a minute.

I start zipping my bag closed, nearly ready to go, when I hear a voice. Dom is in the doorway.

"DaVinci, I've got some great work news," he says as a red jelly doughnut crumb falls from his mouth and into his mug of coffee. "One of the fancy pants painters around town had to cancel on a job for a new build, so my bid was the next one they took."

"What does that mean for me?" I ask him, rubbing the sleep from my eyes.

"It means today's your first day on the job, bub. It's so last minute I have to do a little prep on a Sunday, which I never do. Even in the summer I take my football very seriously. It's the pre-season's pre-season," he says with a smile. "But with two guys it'll be done in no time. Throw on some work clothes and we're outta here."

"Oh. I was thinking I might go to the hospital, if—"

"She's fine. Trust me," Dom cuts in. "Talking to doctors. Listening in on other patients' vacation plans. Eating awful food and getting closer to that transplant. We should only be a few hours anyways."

I look at my backpack filled with boring distractions. Why not spend a few hours doing something else?

"Alright." I shrug.

"That's the spirit. Now toss on some work clothes and let's go."

He turns and walks back to the kitchen.

I look down at the light-green Dom and Son shirt Dom gave me. It's one of three I plan on wearing for the summer. I then look at my shorts that I picked up from a wrinkled heap below my army cot.

They are one of two pairs that I plan on wearing, again, for the length of the summer.

"I think I'm already in my work clothes?"

"Well, perfect, then. Let's hit the road," Dom says from the kitchen. "No time to waste. The early bird gets ringworms, or whatever."

"You holding up okay?" Dom says as he drives his van with his right hand, his left elbow out the window. I realize I've been nervously tapping my fingers on the dashboard for a while now.

"Oh. Yeah, I'm okay."

"I get it, DaVinci. I'm nervous, too," Dom continues. "Family is all we got."

"Speaking of that," I say, tired enough to say just what's on my mind. "Is it true you don't want Nick to paint with you anymore? Nick said that you don't want him to help out because he's kind of color-blind."

Dom puts both hands on the steering wheel, something I am yet to have seen. He looks sort of surprised.

"He tell you that?" he responds, shaking his head. "I mean, I'm his dad—I know he can't tell the difference between red and green. But that doesn't matter, you know? I always told him I could figure out a way to make it work."

It's funny how people can live with one another but still be so far apart.

The van pulls up to a street that is filled with enormous houses, most with pools in the backyard that are encased with screens to shield from bugs and debris. We turn left and are greeted by a green sign that says "The Peerless Pines" in gold cursive writing. There's a tiny little fountain next to it.

"This is where we're working? Does someone important live here?" I ask.

"It's where the who's who of Sugarland come to live. Or at least that's what the brochure says."

Sprinklers are dousing lush lawns with water. Royal palm trees are stuck like squat little gnomes on nearly every corner of the neighborhood. Our blue van rolls down the pristine street, the muffler rattling like two dollars in change going through a dry cycle.

"This new gig is around the corner from Nick's mom's house, actually," Dom says as we pass cul-de-sacs dotted with tiny mansions. "It's coming up on the right here."

We slowly cruise down the freshly paved road, and Dom nods at an off-white house with two sparkling silver SUVs parked in the driveway. The grass in the yard is a bright and vivid green. Sticking out above the white picket fence of the backyard there is a blue-and-yellow roof of a jungle gym/fort/slide contraption. Through the slats of the fence I can see an inflatable kiddie pool right next to it.

"Nick has step-siblings?" I ask, crinkling my forehead.

"Yup," Dom says in a monotone.

"He's never mentioned it," I say, squinting to see if they're in the backyard.

"Yup," Dom says again with even less feeling. I don't see any-one, though, and after another turn we pull into the curving driveway of a light-yellow two-story house with two huge white columns in the front.

Dom parks the car and hops out. "DaVinci!" he calls from the truck bed. "Help me out with these cans.

THE MAP

"OKAY, DAVINCI, THIS IS YOUR SPECIAL TASK," HE SAYS WITH A PROUD look. In the center of the room is a stack of drop cloths and a tower of rolls of blue painter's tape. "You've got one of the most important jobs. We only want to paint the walls, so go along all the ceilings and baseboards and windows and apply this tape to the edges."

"So I'm *not* painting then?" I ask.

"Look at it as building character. This is almost as important as actually painting."

"And this character building still pays ten bucks an hour?" I ask, raising my eyebrows.

"You know it."

"Okay. I'll try," I say, caving in. "I don't really know what I'm doing, though."

"Well, my man, I've got good news—nobody knows what they're doing!" Dom says with a laugh, giving me a hearty pat on the back. He takes a roll of tape and demonstrates how to tape off a corner. "I'll come check on you in an hour or so."

Dom heads back toward the kitchen as I pick up a roll of blue tape and head to the corner of the room. I sit down on the hardwood floor. I can feel the rolled-up journal in my back pocket.

I open it up and start flipping through all the pages my mom numbered by hand, skimming entries on Purple Gallinules and Limpkins. Once I reach the very end, I can see that the last page is stuck to the back cover.

"Huh," I mutter to myself. I guess I hadn't noticed it before.

I carefully peel it back, making sure not to rip any pages. There's a map taped to the inside of the back cover. I try to make sense of it all, but there's no map key or anything. It's drawn by hand, and it seems like it's a chain of islands surrounded by wetlands.

Looking closer, I see that the water is shaded blue with a scribbly ballpoint pen. On various parts of the map there are drawings of birds. In the center is a bird with a bright orange-and-black curled beak—perfect for digging into the shell of a snail.

"This has to be where we'll find our Snail Kite," I whisper. "But where is this?"

Luckily, I know the person who knows.

ISLANDS

"ANYBODY HOME?" I SAY, KNOCKING ON THE DOOR TO MY MOM'S HOSPITAL room.

I take a step into the doorway and see a nurse at the bedside, carefully drawing enough blood to fill up a couple of vials. Mondays are always busy in hospitals.

"G!" says Mom with a startled look on her face. I can tell she's surprised. I would be too, I guess, if unexpected guests arrived while blood was actively being sucked out of my arm.

"We'll be done here in one second, my friend," says the nurse.

"Gotcha. I won't stay long. Dom dropped me off while he went to get more blue tape. It's only my second day and I finished three rolls already. He said I'm too quick so he's giving me the afternoon off," I say.

"Well, seeing you is always a treat," Mom says. Her eyes are bloodshot and her hair is matted from being in a hospital bed nonstop. She seems kind of groggy and disoriented.

I look at the wall above her bed. It's now filled with cards and notes from long-distance friends and family. The last time I was here there weren't any, and now they're stretching the length of the room.

"All set," says the nurse, finished with the blood draw. She snaps off a pair of latex gloves and washes her hands in the sink in my mom's room. "Take care now."

I walk to the window and open the curtains, letting in the afternoon sunlight.

"Sorry for just popping by. Figured even seeing you for a little while would be nice," I say, standing next to her bed. "Are . . . is everything okay?"

"Oh, I'm fine, bud," she answers, looking to the corner of the ceiling. "It's simply impossible to get more than four straight hours of sleep in this place, there's always people coming in and out all the time."

She takes a sip of water from her plastic Florida Clinic mug. Her hands are lightly shaking.

"But it could be worse. I'm grateful to be here," she says. "But seriously, who comes to Florida to just sit in the air-conditioning?"

I try to muster up a fake laugh as she chuckles with a tiny sniffle. "Well, you'll be happy to know we almost saw a Snail Kite. At least I think," I say, hoping talking about birds might cheer her up.

"Yeah? Where'd you see it?" she says, a spark hinting in her eyes.

"Behind Dom's," I say. "Lou actually told us about this contest to find one. The winner gets five thousand dollars."

"Lou?" Mom asks.

Classic Mom. Way more interested in my making friends than

five *thousand* dollars. But then it clicks—I realize I haven't talked with my mom since Lou showed up at the house.

"Lou lives not too far from Dom, but we met here at the hospital the other day. Her dad's waiting for a transplant, too," I explain. "I'll introduce her sometime. She totally loved hearing about your birding journal. Wait! That reminds me . . ."

I grab the journal and flip it open to the map on the last page.

"Do you remember where this is? It seems like some islands somewhere, but there's nothing written on it."

As I hand the journal to my mom, I can see life instantly returning to her eyes. She looks like her old self again.

"Of course, I know what this is. This is a very special place, Graham. A historical landmark, even."

"Oh yeah?" I answer. "Is it like a sunken ship or one of those bottomless swimming holes I've seen online?"

"Very funny," she replies. "It's the Salvato Memorial Marsh. It was dedicated the year your father and I graduated high school."

I can tell memories are flickering behind her tired eyes.

"We went out there all the time. Your dad met some of the people doing the conservation work, so he knew the best spots. He was so excited that one of his favorite places was going to be protected from bulldozers and pavement."

"Is it still there?"

"I'd hope so. Probably the only place around Sugarland that won't be turned into fancy houses. There are parts that really feel like a wild jungle," she continues. "The last time I was there, your father and I went out the day high school ended and had a bonfire with friends. It's actually the site of our first kiss."

My cheeks flame red. "That's disgusting."

Mom laughs. She brings the journal closer toward her and studies the faded old map.

"Your dad drew this map. He always knew the way and I always got lost, that's why he drew this for me," she says, studying the map taped inside the journal. "He swore he saw a Snail Kite there once and was always convinced we'd find one there for my journal. He never let me give up on the dreams I had as a little girl."

"Really? That's cool."

I lean over to look at the map more, too. I didn't realize my dad was such a good artist.

"I wish I could remember which one is our special island."

She leans back, deep in a memory that's far from IV drugs and heart-rate monitors.

"It was surrounded by cypress trees, and your dad always said it was our secret place. Sometimes I can close my eyes and go there in my mind," she says. "That final time we went there we planted a magnolia tree next to a black olive tree. They were our babies, we said. There for us whenever we'd want to go back. Now if I could only remember where . . ."

Her forehead wrinkles as she looks intently, tracing the islands with her pointer finger. Mom picks up a pen and circles an area with a bunch of small islands. She then draws a looping, mazelike trail on the map, winding around islands and going through tiny waterways. Her hand is still shaky, but I can tell she's trying to hold it still.

"Here. At least, *somewhere* in here."

Mom smiles at me. I can't help but wonder if finishing this journal and finding this bird will make a difference to her. That it could somehow help her find a new heart.

Mom always says birds deliver messages. Maybe this one will deliver something more. A miracle, maybe.

Suddenly the machine next to us starts making lots of loud beeps, and outside our room a light on the ceiling begins to flash.

"Mom?"

ROBB WITH TWO B'S

"Sounds like we're having a little party in here," says a nurse briskly walking into the room. He's in light blue scrubs and seems a bit older than my mom, a lifetime cured in the Florida sun. His short hair is going gray on the sides, and he has thin wire-framed glasses.

"You tell your heart to quit acting up," he says as he examines the heart-rate monitor next to my mom's bed. His voice is calm and peaceful.

"There we go," he says as he pushes a few buttons. The lights and beeps all stop—at least for now.

"G, this is Robb, with two *b*'s. Believe it or not, we went to the same high school. I was four years behind him."

"Pleasure to meet you, Graham," he says, studying the screen a moment longer before turning back to me. "Your mom's our favorite patient. Her room is where I come when I need a break from the break room!"

Mom blushes a bit.

"Aren't you supposed to say everybody is your favorite patient?" she asks.

"Whoever told you that obviously hadn't worked three straight days of sixteen-hour shifts," Robb answers, flashing a smile. "But vacation starts next week! Home to see Mom in Cuba. Be right back, Lindsay."

He grabs my mom's plastic Florida Clinic mug and heads into the hallway toward what I'd call a solid B+ ice machine.

"You've done it again," I say, pulling up a chair next to her bed.

My mom becoming fast friends with entire floors of nurses is nothing new. She's always found a way to win over the hearts of hospital staff. In Buffalo, I'm pretty sure she was invited to the weddings of three separate nurses in the last year alone.

"Everybody here is great," Mom says. She gazes out of her window that overlooks palm trees and parking lots. "What are you doing this evening, G? Seems like it will be a nice night out."

"Um, I'm not really sure," I answer.

"Maybe you and Nick could do something. You know, get to know each other better. He seems like a nice guy."

Robb enters the room again, saving me from having to answer. My mom's cup is filled with cold water and ice pellets. As he hands it to her my phone buzzes with a text from Lou.

> Wanna meet us at Swansen's??? My dad says it's our treat! Meet us at four?

"Oh, weird timing. This is Lou, who I was telling you about. Sounds like she and her dad are headed to Swansen's."

"Swansen's? I can already tell she's my kind of gal," Mom jokes. "Go! Have some fun. I'll have to meet this Lou person. Maybe me and her dad will be out of here sooner than later. We'll all do milkshakes."

I give a half-hearted smile. Sometimes it's hard to think of the future when it doesn't feel certain.

"And Graham, if you want to know a real local's secret, at Swansen's you've got to ask for your burger to be made 'Rudy Style,'" says Robb.

"What's that?"

"You'll have to see for yourself," says the nurse.

"Will do," I reply, walking over to hug Mom goodbye.

"See you soon, G," Mom says as she brings me in close for a hug. I close my eyes, trying not to listen to the offbeat beeping of machines. Mom rubs my back, and I feel the IV tube resting on my shoulder for just a second. It feels like it weighs seventy-five tons.

"See you soon, Mom."

"I love you."

"I love you, too."

JOB SECURITY

I'VE BEEN WALKING A LOT IN SUGARLAND, WHICH IS COOL. I HAVEN'T BEEN listening to music either. I've been enjoying wandering around deep in thought, I guess.

Not only have I ventured back behind Dom's place, but I've explored around the hospital. My phone says it is barely over a mile from the hospital to Swansen's, and in that time I have passed five restaurants, three gas stations advertising sales on energy drinks, and some kind of deep-freeze frozen yogurt place designed to look like a futuristic snack spaceship.

I'm always fascinated by things like hospitals being such close walking distance from fast-food joints. Sometimes they're even in the lobby. I mean isn't all this stuff, like, wildly bad for you?

And I mean it's not like I enjoy kale more than the next guy, but of all the places where they should be trying to make us healthy, wouldn't you think it would be a hospital? A place dedicated to health and healing?

I guess I get it, though.

When life gets hard, food can be comforting. Everybody just wants to forget about it all and eat a cheeseburger.

RUDY STYLE

"GRAHAM!" LOU CHIRPS FROM THE PASSENGER SEAT OF A LIGHT-GREEN SUV with Florida license plates as it pulls up to a spot in the Swansen's lot. Lou and her dad park and get out, walking over to the picnic table where I've been sitting for a couple of minutes.

"Graham, this is my dad," she says.

"Nice to meet you, young man," says her dad. We shake hands, though his seems kind of lifeless and weak. I can see his eyes are tired, almost the same as my mom's. "I'm so glad Lou has found a friend."

"Nice meeting you, too," I say.

He pulls out two twenty-dollar bills and hands them to Lou.

"Everything's on me. You guys enjoy it," he says. "Lou, how about you getting mine before we leave? I think I have to take a quick nap in the car, kiddo."

"Sure thing, Dad," she says. "We'll be by the tables over there."

I watch as he slowly climbs into the back seat of their car and shuts the door behind him. I figure he's had a day of doing the same thing as my mom: tons of tests, followed by drawing blood, then countless doctor visits. At least he's able to do it outside of the hospital.

"Everything okay?" I ask.

"Yeah, we're okay. It's been a long day," Lou answers.

She tosses her backpack on the table and sits next to me at one of Swansen's picnic tables. Each one is shaded with a big red-white-and-blue-striped umbrella.

As Lou gets settled, a chipper Swansen's server comes to the table. She's wearing a blue visor and a button that says "Ask Me About Our Takeaway Pint of Ranch Dressing!"

"Howdy, everybody. How're we doin' this afternoon?" she says.

"Great! My friend here is going to go first. I'm not ready yet," Lou says, staring at the menu.

"Okay. I'll have a number four with a small chocolate-and-peanut-butter shake," I say.

I clear my throat and lower my voice, a little worried this whole "secret menu" is just a trick that the locals play on tourists.

"And can that burger be . . . 'Rudy Style'?"

Time feels like it slows down as the server looks up at me from her tablet. It's like she's seeing if I belong in the club. Her stern face is like those judges at the dog show they always broadcast on Thanksgiving, almost as if everything I've done in my life up to this point is being judged at this very moment. I can feel a few beads of sweat forming on the very top of my head.

"No problem at all," the server says, going back to a bright smile. "That's my favorite, too."

"Can I get two more of those?" Lou asks. "One to go, please."

The server nods and says, "Coming right up."

"What did we order?" Lou asks, when she's gone.

"I have absolutely no idea," I say with a smile. But for a split second I feel like I might belong in Sugarland.

LONG VIEW

"THESE ARE FOR YOU," LOU SAYS, OFFERING A PAIR OF BLACK PLASTIC binoculars with her left hand, the other clutching her Swansen's milkshake. "I searched online for some of the best brands out there. Then I found these in a gas station. Did you know binoculars could be so expensive?"

"Really?"

"Totally. Some people pay thousands for a pair of—"

"No, I mean, are you sure these are for me? I don't have anything for you, though. I feel kind of bad. I should have a gift for you, too."

"They're yours. Really," Lou says, shoving the binoculars at me again.

"Dang. Thanks, Lou."

I put down my milkshake and take one more bite of my burger that's covered in some kind of fantastic spicy-yet-sweet secret sauce.

It's like Thousand Island dressing that found a couple bonus, sassy islands on the map.

I bring the binoculars up to my eyes and peer at the Swansen's menu in front of us. It's all huge and magnified and instantly gives me a headache.

"Whoa," I say.

I spin to the right a bit and focus on a group of trees. I can see every tiny pine cone on each tree, plus a few squirrels playfully scrambling between them all.

"The guy who sold them to me said you can see something from five hundred yards away," Lou says as she sips her milkshake. She puts her dad's food in her bag. "Supposedly it's like having hawk vision. Or at least some kind of bird of prey."

"Bird fact: most falcons actually have awful vision and get Lasik eye surgery done at a young age," I say with a smile.

Lou groans.

I keep scanning and suddenly see the real estate billboard up close. My stomach drops as I see the trees where my mom and I went searching for the Snail Kite. I remember the way my chest felt tight as we left with a team of paramedics.

I quickly pull the binoculars away from my face.

"Do they work?"

"Oh yeah, they're great. I might just take a little break for now," I say, putting them down next to my milkshake. I nervously lean forward and take a sip, still able to feel the adrenaline I had from the other day. It's like I'll never be able to look at that patch of trees again without thinking about something awful. And, unfortunately, there's just too many places scattered throughout my life where this is the case.

"I also downloaded some birding apps," she says, holding her phone in front of me. "You can actually type in 'Snail Kite' right here and it'll show you if anybody has spotted one recently."

We look at a few marked locations on a map of southern Florida.

"Look at this! It says there's a possible Snail Kite sighting not even three miles from here," Lou says, excited. "Someplace called the Salvato Marsh."

"Whoa, really?" I say. I pull out my mom's journal, excited. "My mom's book has a map of that place!"

I open up to the hand-drawn map and point at the set of islands my mom circled.

"She said my dad was sure a Snail Kite lived somewhere around here."

Lou zooms in on the map on her phone, though it's tough to see much on the tiny screen. But soon I can see distinct islands that look like the ones my mom circled. Her map is a portion from the dead center of the nature preserve.

"This will be the place where we find our bird," Lou says. "It isn't far at all. I think we should go check it out."

"You mean right this minute?" I say. "Maybe we'll go another day."

"Who knows what's going to happen on another day, Graham Dodds," Lou says, gathering up her trash and tossing it in a nearby trash can. "We gotta go now."

But before I can even stand up, two people come and stand behind me, casting long, menacing shadows over our table.

A WILD GROUSE CHASE

"Well, look who it is: two people who are about to lose five grand," says a voice.

It's Nick's buddies from before. I look behind them, but Nick doesn't seem to be with them this time.

"I thought you said you had a fancy boat to get to," Lou says, spinning her legs to the outside of the picnic table bench.

"That's the good thing about fancy boats, like ours. They're always right there on the dock whenever you need 'em," says the shorter one, who I think said his name was DJ.

He stands on his tiptoes and leans forward, peering over my shoulder at my dad's map. I try to hunch my shoulders over the journal in an attempt to block his view. After all, there's valuable Snail Kite information on this map.

"What do you guys want?" Lou says, standing up. She's nervously fidgeting with one of her friendship bracelets.

"Me and Zane only want the same thing as you: the cash," DJ says, sounding like a bratty kid waiting on their allowance.

"Well, for your information, we're not just doing this for the cash," Lou shoots back. "We happen to love birds."

"Good. 'Cause we happen to hate 'em," says DJ's older brother Zane, once again cracking a piece of gum in his mouth.

"You hate birds?" I ask.

"Rats of the sky," says DJ. "You ever had a bird blast a huge turd on your head? They are my sworn enemies."

His eyes are still fixed on the journal in front of me.

"If I see one, I'm gonna take a picture of me launching a rock at it," Zane says with a snorting laugh. "Contest doesn't say the bird can't be injured in the photo, right?"

The two boys laugh, and Lou takes a step toward them. I can tell she's getting upset. She's slowly beginning to look like one of the angrier emojis.

"If you hate birds so much, then why are you doing this contest?" she asks.

"Do you know how big a flat-screen TV we'll be able to buy with that kind of cash?" Zane says. "Bigger than the wall we'll hang it on."

"But, you know, we've had horrible luck finding this snail-sucker," DJ says, typing something into his phone. "And it looks like you've got a book there with a lot of clues."

Zane walks up to the side of our picnic table and stands close to me, glaring at me with a menacing stare. Lou looks up at him, then back at DJ.

"Maybe it's a little harder than you thought to find a bird you know nothing about," Lou muses, crossing her arms.

"Most definitely. And before running into you bird freaks we had no idea about birding apps or that marsh," DJ continues. He pauses for a moment and then shows his brother his phone's screen. "But it looks like we hit the jackpot, bro. See that? Right here it says there's a sighting today. That means there's five thousand bucks flying around over there at this very moment."

DJ's face gets serious as he inches closer to us.

"And the only thing that's standing in our way is finding that bird, with that map," he says.

I slam the journal shut and stuff it into my backpack, sliding it underneath the calligraphy book I'd brought to the hospital. But the taller brother, Zane, grabs one of the straps of my backpack.

"I can take this off your hands," he says. I grab the other strap and jerk it back toward me. We struggle back and forth, the seams of my backpack beginning to tear.

"Stop! That's ours!" Lou shouts as she grabs the bag with me. But the other brother joins in, and soon it's a tug-of-war.

"Quit fighting. It'll be easier if you give us the map," DJ says. Lou and I dig our heels into the grass, but they're obviously stronger than both of us. My pulse is pounding in my ears. I hate confrontation—like, really hate it.

"You're never getting our map," Lou shouts.

But I get an idea. I reach a hand into my bag and grab the book that's on the top of my mom's journal.

"Here! Take it!" I say, pulling it out and tossing it high in the air.

Zane lets go of the backpack to reach for the falling book, and I rip the backpack from DJ. "Run!"

Lou and I make a dash for her parents' car, my pulse still pounding. We dodge servers carrying trays of hot dogs and French fries and begin to maneuver through the parking lot. I turn to glance back and can see Nick's buddies leafing through the book, looking for a map but only finding page after page of beautifully swooping letters and words.

"Enjoy the calligraphy!" I shout back.

As we approach the green SUV, I realize I'm clutching the bag with my mom's journal to my chest so tightly my knuckles have turned white.

"See ya in the marsh, losers," Zane calls after us, shoving the book in a trash can nearby.

I zip my backpack shut as we finally get to Lou's car.

"You're right, about not knowing what could come another day," I say, still out of breath. "Plus, now we have to find this bird before those guys. The race is on."

"That's the spirit," Lou says. She swings open the passenger door, disturbing her dad's nap. "Now, rise and shine, cupcake! We're going to a marsh."

GARY AND LORETTA

"You have your backpack, right sweetie? I'll be here when you're ready," mumbles Lou's dad as he reclines the driver's seat in his SUV. He tips a baseball cap over his eyes as the sounds of sports talk radio come through the open windows. Even though I feel a tiny bit guilty for making him drive us over, I'm glad he's getting to rest.

We get to a visitor center for the marsh, which has a couple of restrooms and an information booth that's closed for the night. There's a small chalkboard propped up on the counter, reading:

"Back at 8 a.m. $5 Map Donation Box Here ⇨"

I reach into my pocket and pull out ten dollars I got from working for Dom. I drop it into a thin slot on the top of a wooden box and take two maps.

"This seems like an amusement park for dangerous reptiles," I say, glancing at the warnings plastered all over the map. There's a long list of animals that have been seen in the area: gators, boa constrictors, wild boar, panthers, and spiders the size of frisbees.

"Looks like there's a trail we can take that makes a little loop," says Lou.

With our maps unfolded, we head toward a mulch path that leads to the start of a wooden walkway. Huge branches covered in hanging moss dangle overhead. We haven't been walking long, and it feels like dinosaurs are about to leap out at us at any second. It's like another world.

"Graham Dodds Bird Fact," I say over my shoulder, still looking up. "The Great Blue Heron was named after someone's friend Sharon."

"Ha! I like that," says a voice from behind me that is definitely not Lou.

We turn around to see an old man wearing a birding outfit similar to Lou's. His hair is white and fluffy, like a cloud. He has a large bucket hat that matches his tan vest and shorts, and his white socks are pulled up high, nearly to his knees.

"Sorry to eavesdrop, but I figured you can never know too many bird facts," says the man. A pair of binoculars is around his neck, and in his right hand is a wooden walking stick that almost looks like a twisted wizard staff. "I'm Gary."

"Nice to meet you," I say.

"You scaring these fine young kids off, Gary?" says a woman appearing from the direction of the marsh's visitor center. Her outfit is identical to Gary's.

"Wouldn't be the first time." Gary chuckles.

"Not at all. I'm Lou and this is Graham."

The woman takes off her wide-brimmed sun blocking hat and dabs her forehead with a white bandana. She has a kind, round face and curly hair that's a few different shades of gray. Her light-brown eyes match her skin tone, and she's wearing some heavy-duty hiking boots.

"I'm Loretta. It's so good to see you both out here," she says between sips of water. "It thrills me to see young people finding a love for nature."

Gary takes the backpack he's wearing and puts it on the ground in front of his feet. It's covered with patches that are sewn on.

"What are all those?" Lou asks.

"We're on our Big Year," Gary says proudly.

"What's that?" I blurt, before realizing what a ridiculous question it probably sounds like. Clearly, a Big Year is a big deal.

Gary smiles widely and says, "It's where birders buckle down and try to find as many species as they can in twelve months. You pull out all the stops, no plane ticket too expensive. All these patches are countries we've visited since February in search of our lifers."

"Lifer?" I ask, looking at all the patches. There's one that says Trinidad in bold colors, and another in the shape of Mexico. I recognize the red-and-white maple leaf of the Canadian flag, but there are a couple more that I can't place. I wonder what sorts of birds they saw in those places.

"A lifer is a first-time sighting for a birder. A species someone hasn't seen but has been seeking out," Loretta explains, but her eyes quickly dart to the right. "Gary, did you catch that?"

Her eyes are on a cluster of trees in a sandy spot just off the wooden walkway.

"Missed it, what'd ya see?" he says, squinting his eyes.

"A Florida Scrub-Jay is down at the base of that tall scrub oak tree. There might even be a few of them," Loretta says.

"Really? I was just reading about them in my book," Lou says. "I think they might be my favorite."

"You've got good taste," says Loretta. "They're really smart—they bury thousands of acorns in the fall and then dig them up in the winter and spring."

"So, they're like a genius bird," Lou says with a triumphant head nod.

"Ha! Well, maybe. They're also real friendly," Gary adds. "They'll eat peanuts if you toss a few on the ground near their feet. Heck, so will I."

Lou and I laugh as Loretta rolls her eyes and bats him with her hat. Gary seems a little kooky, but in a fun, bird-loving grandpa kind of way.

"You can hear the Scrub-Jays by their sharp little squawk of a call," Loretta says.

In the distance, I can hear the birds chatting with one another, chirping in the late-day sun. I close my eyes and imagine what they might be saying, if maybe they're talking about us as well. Whatever they're saying, there's a lot of it.

"As you might've noticed, Scrub-Jays are quite the talkative species," Loretta adds, breaking my reverie. It's almost as though she can read my thoughts.

"My mom is a big birder," I admit. "She thinks they deliver messages."

"If that's so, Scrub-Jays deliver messages of the long-winded variety," Gary pipes up.

"Takes one to know one," Loretta says as she puts her hat back on and adjusts the brim.

Lou giggles. "I think they're fabulous."

"Lou, why don't you and I go see if they're hungry?" says Loretta. "I happen to have some locally sourced peanuts, their favorite."

"Deal," Lou says with a smile.

I watch as they head down the path toward the Scrub-Jay, and even from far away I hear Lou's delighted squeal as Scrub-Jays begin to land near her feet.

I can't help but notice it's different from how I spend most of my days: waiting around for answers that never come while usually eating cold soup.

Now, I didn't really expect to say this, but I think I like this birding stuff more than I anticipated.

Out here I get the feeling that you never know how your day might turn out. It's kind of nice in a way. I mean, we barely started searching before meeting interesting people like Gary and Loretta, and everywhere I look there's something new. A tree I've never seen before. Some kind of animal that looks like a terrifying dinosaur. Everything is constantly changing. If you're in the right place, at the right time, something magical might happen.

I have no idea what's about to happen next, but for the first time ever, I think . . . I might actually like it.

The Fossil

Gary and I grab a seat on a bench made from recycled plastic as Loretta and Lou are kneeling at the base of a tall tree, small snacking birds bouncing around them.

"Has anyone told you about the dangers of this swamp yet?" Gary asks me.

"Like snakes?"

Gary shakes his head no.

"There's something in here that makes pythons look like tadpoles. Something even scarier."

I raise my eyebrows.

"They say it escaped from a movie set decades ago," Gary says, his voice getting low and serious as if he's sharing a ghost story. "They were filming a movie called *River of the Fossil Monsters*. One of the last great movies before computers took it all over. About an ancient alligator that kept growing for centuries."

I try to think if I've seen it, but it doesn't sound familiar.

"The gator that got out was fifteen feet long at first. But over the years it's kept on growing and growing. A park ranger told me they saw it three years ago and it had to be as long as a school bus, if not bigger."

I gulp. "Does it have a name?"

"The locals call it 'the Fossil,'" Gary says with wide eyes. "Some people say it's got to be a hundred years old by now. Big enough to eat a horse."

"Whoa," I say.

My heart skips a beat. Was that what we saw the other day? Didn't Nick say that these channels were all connected? Was I about to be eaten by a gator the size of a bus?

"So, if you're ever out in the marshes looking for birds, be careful, be prepared," Gary says, finally leaning back on the bench. "The Fossil will be."

I feel my palms begin to sweat as I imagine the roar of a gator as it swims near me. I shake the thought from my mind. After all, the odds of getting eaten by a gator are low.

The odds of finding a mythical swamp monster? Even smaller. Right?

LOST AND FOUND

"GRAHAM, GUESS WHAT? FLORIDA SCRUB-JAYS ARE ENDEMIC," LOU SAYS, bouncing back toward me and Gary.

"Is that a blood thing? Do they need to eat a candy bar?" I ask.

Lou rolls her eyes. "It means you can only find this species of jay in Florida—like me!"

Lou is beaming. I haven't known her long, but I can tell she is in her element.

"The good news is that they're usually easy to find," Loretta says, catching up with Lou. "Their way of life is still threatened, but they keep on adapting."

"I think Loretta has been birding longer than anyone ever," Lou says with enthusiasm. "She said she started when she was about twelve, same as us. And now you're how old?"

Lou looks up at the woman, her gray hair extra-curly from the humidity.

"Old enough to know you're not getting an answer to that question," she says with a chuckle. "I have to say, I love this place—our home base between birding adventures. After all these years this marsh never disappoints."

She sits next to Gary, who lovingly gives her a pat on the knee and a kiss on the cheek.

"Tell 'em about Parsley, honey," Gary says.

"What's Parsley?" I ask. "Other than something for potatoes."

"Oh, they don't want to hear about that."

"Sure we do," Lou replies.

"It's how Loretta got her start with birding," Gary answers, clasping his hands over his belly like walrus flippers.

"Tell us! Please?" Lou says.

I listen as the Scrub-Jays finish up their conversation and begin flying off, a scurrying cloud of wings and feathers.

"Oh, she belonged to my best friend's older sister," Loretta begins. "A bright yellow parakeet with a red beak and a hot pink ring around its neck, so it looked like it was always wearing a necklace."

"Nice," Lou says.

"She'd always fly around the house and land on your shoulder, and if she liked you, she'd eat a peanut out of your hand," Loretta says, holding her hand out for an imaginary bird. "But one day she got out, the poor thing. She was hiding in a jacket someone was wearing and flew off."

"What happened?" I ask her, worried I already know the answer.

"Well, we went out searching every day for weeks. We tried to set up other birds to call her back, and left out open cages full of food," Loretta says. "But we never found Parsley. My friend's mom said it was an accident, and accidents happen. It's sad, but I like to think something good came of it in the end. That's where my love for birding started."

"That's special. Thanks for sharing," Lou says. "What do you think ever happened to the parakeet?"

"I like to think she made it to Brazil, perched on the shoulder of an energetic samba dancer," Loretta smiles.

"Well, we'll keep an eye out for birds with hot pink rings around their neck," Lou says. "We can take a picture for you. We're actually searching for a Snail Kite ourselves."

We hand Loretta the poster for the contest.

"It makes this old heart of mine happy to see young people get into birding," says Gary. "I found it late in life and think people could learn great things from being lifelong birders. Imagine if I'd started at their age? The places I could've explored with knees that actually work!"

"You'd probably be growing feathers by now," Loretta jokes.

Loretta keeps reading the fine print for the contest and takes another sip from her water bottle. It has a sticker that says: Save the Salvato Marsh!

"What do you think you'll write for the essay portion on your Snail Kite entry?" Loretta says, handing the flyer back to Lou.

"Wait, essay portion?" Lou asks, her forehead wrinkling.

"That seems like half the fun. It says it right here, you submit a photo, but also have two hundred fifty words to describe what it meant to you," says Loretta. "Right here in the fine print."

"How'd we miss that before?" I ask Lou.

"I'm more of a 'take action now, read the fine print later' kind of gal," Lou says.

"It'll be a great challenge then," Loretta says with a grin. She reaches into her backpack and hands Lou a spare bucket hat. It has the logo for the Salvato Marsh on the front, and a wavy brim that goes around in a circle. "Here, take this for good luck."

"Really?" Lou asks with wide eyes.

"Really. And Graham, a patch from my mom back home in Haiti. I got this when I saw a Hispaniolan Trogon on my birthday. The national bird. Maybe it'll bring you good luck, too."

Loretta hands me the patch of the red-and-blue flag, and I can already sense the powerful bird magic that it holds.

I hear a splash in the water nearby and watch as a few turtles slide off a log.

"You kids have a boat by any chance?" Gary asks. "You can see a lot more of the marsh from the water. That's how you find the good stuff."

My mind immediately thinks of Nick, how he took his boat and ditched us.

"And kids, don't get discouraged. There are a lot of birds out there, you don't have to know every one of them," Gary says. "I don't think I've ever correctly identified a bird call in my whole life, but I'm not going to stop trying!"

We laugh as a pair of buzzing wasps float past us.

"Well, I'd say it's almost my bedtime, Loretta May," says Gary. "You ready to go, my love?"

"Sounds good," agrees Loretta. "It was a pleasure meeting you both. Hopefully we'll see you around."

"You too," Lou replies. "And thanks."

The two head back toward the visitor center, holding hands and keeping their eyes up for any possible lifers soaring by.

"So, how do we get a boat?" Lou says. "I think maybe my cousin has one we could liberate, but I'm not sure how we'd get it to your house."

"Liberate?"

"Borrow."

"Ah yes, steal," I say, finally understanding.

"But my parents kind of worry a lot. I'm not sure they'd be of any help with it."

"Where could we buy a boat? How much does something like that even cost?"

We sit in silence for a second, both of us trying not to admit that we need Nick.

"Hey! Sugar Bear!" shouts a voice from the parking lot. It's coming from Lou's car.

"We're coming, Dad. Be right there," she shouts back.

I burst out in laughter.

"Sugar Bear? Are those native to Florida, too?" I say with a mischievous smile.

"That's it, you're walking home," Lou jokes. She playfully punches me in my shoulder as we start heading back to her dad.

And I know she's joking, but you know what? Even with the swampy air, and the brutal sun, I'm not sure I would mind.

I'm not ready for the day to end.

THE ROOM AGAIN

You know how sometimes you're in a dream and halfway through you know you're dreaming? Like, everything is too ridiculous or too surreal to be real life, but you can't stop what's happening?

Right now, I'm in My Waiting Room, but in the middle of the room there's a big map. Like when you're in a mall and there's a map of the stores with a big star that says You Are Here. It's exactly like that, only it looks a lot like the map I found in my mom's journal.

I stare at the map, studying to see if this might finally be a way out of this room. I try to chart a map toward the middle and head off.

I start walking and the fake pleather chairs start turning into bushes. The gross paint on the walls has been replaced by tree bark. I take turn after turn, ducking under branches and stepping over roots.

But every time I think I'm getting close to the center, I always end up back at the start. I start running through the maze of islands, but I only get lost and spat back out. I start sprinting, trying to get out. I'm sweating and I just want nothing more than to leave this place forever. But I can't. And I spend the whole night—day—whatever this is—running.

I finally open my eyes.

Peerless Pines

"What time is it?" says Nick in a half-yawn. His head is mostly covered up by a pillow.

"Almost nine," I say, barely looking his way. "Did you know the Salvato Marsh was so close to your backyard?"

The birds have been chirping for a while, and our room is getting hot from the sunlight that's directly hitting the side of the house. I'm on my army cot and Nick is still snoozing across the room from me. I can smell Dom's coffee brewing in the kitchen as I keep studying the paper map I got from the visitors center. It's unfolded before me and I have the hand-drawn map from my mom's book next to it. It looks nearly identical. My dad was pretty great at drawing, it turns out. I wonder what else he was good at?

Nick groans and slowly emerges from underneath the pillow. I throw a pillow over my maps, careful to not give Nick any tips.

"That marsh basically *is* my backyard," Nick says, reaching for a glass of water on his nightstand. "We almost got there the other day, before we turned around."

"And then you figured you'd take those other jerks instead of us the next time?"

Nick doesn't say anything. Instead, he walks to the bathroom just down the hall and starts to brush his teeth.

"Are you using your boat today? Could we borrow it?" I call out. He peeks his head into the bedroom doorway with a toothbrush hanging out of his mouth. His face is contorted, and he gives me a glare with worried, bushy eyebrows.

"Nobody elthe can drive ith, thorry," Nick says. I hear him shuffle back to the bathroom and spit out a mouthful of toothpaste. "My dad made me take a safety lesson with him and everything."

Ugh. I hear the faucet turn on then off as Nick comes back in the room.

"Don't you have football practice anyways? You won't be around."

"Wrong. Half the time I'm supposed to be in practice I'm not. I don't even like football."

"Then where can we get a boat like yours? We have to have one."

"My dad found ours. It was basically garbage, but he fixed it up," Nick says, beginning to load up his backpack with bug spray and sunscreen. "Maybe look online or something, or at a dock if people are selling."

"I guess we could," I say, feeling pretty defeated. I head to the bathroom and brush my teeth as well. For some reason I remember what Lou had to say yesterday, about not knowing when you might get another day to do something.

"You know you should painth withh me and yourt dad somthethime. I thhhingk you'd like kit," I say to Nick, leaning into the hallway with my mouth full of toothpaste.

"Whatever," he murmurs. I spit and rinse with a sip of water.

"I mean, it's even in that new Peerless Pines place. We go right by your mom's house on the way to work. We could say hello," I say, stashing my toothbrush back in the medicine cabinet. I look in the mirror, waiting for a response, but it never comes. In the reflection I see Nick rush through the hallway, his footsteps muffled by the shaggy green carpet. Then I hear the back sliding door open and slam shut.

Hey, at least I tried, right?

LIBERATION STATION

I'VE BEEN SITTING IN MY MOM'S ROOM FOR AN HOUR. SHE'S BEEN ASLEEP since I got here. I haven't heard back from Lou today, even though I texted her first thing. After meeting Gary and Loretta yesterday, I'm ready to keep up our birding momentum.

"Psst. Graham," comes a voice to my right.

I look over and see Lou's head peeking through the doorway. I glance back at my mom, who's still asleep, and slowly tiptoe out of the room.

"Any luck on the boat?" Lou asks immediately.

"How are you doing? Is everything okay with your dad? I didn't hear from you, so this morning—"

"Yeah, yeah, yeah, we're good," Lou says, kind of rolling her eyes. "Focus on what's important, Graham. Liberating Nick's boat."

"Well, that could be tough. I don't think anyone in the world could pry that boat away from him," I explain.

We're interrupted by a message on the hallway loudspeakers.

"Code blue, code blue," the voice says quickly.

"What's that mean?" I say to Lou.

"I don't think we want to know."

Several hospital staff members rush down the hall and around a corner. We stay put, right by the doorway leading to my mom's room.

"Graham?" comes a scratchy voice.

Mom's awake.

"Wanna meet my mom?" I ask Lou.

"Absolutely."

We head into the room and both stand on either side of my mom's bed.

"Oh wow, we've got company. I would've worn my good night-gown," Mom rasps, taking a sip of water. "You must be the infamous Lou."

"And you must be the infamous Graham's Mom. Lou Watkins, pleased to meet you."

Lou reaches out and takes my mom's outstretched right hand. My mom squeezes both our hands, an old habit of hers.

"How's your day going? If you want me to cause a distraction so you can bust out of here, you just say the word," Lou says to her.

Mom chuckles.

"Ooh, I like you. No need for that yet," she says with a wink. "How is your family? Graham told me you're here with your father."

"We're doing okay, I'd say."

"How long has your dad been sick?" Mom asks.

"As long as I can remember, I guess."

I nod my head in agreement. Even though I can remember before, once things change the years tend to feel a lot longer.

"Graham said you're from Sugarland," Mom continues.

"Yes, ma'am," Lou says. "I hear you're a Florida bird yourself."

Mom sighs. "Yes, but lately we've been migrating from place to place with high hopes that our worries will soon be behind us."

Lou nods, her face serious. "My dad is finally a 2, after being a 3 for forever."

"Well, I hope for all the best for your flock too. Really," Mom says, still holding onto Lou's hand. "I don't know if Graham has mentioned it, but I like to say that it all happens for a reason. That usually helps me during tough times."

"It all happens for a reason," Lou repeats with a grin. "Mind if I use it?"

Mom smiles. "I'd honestly prefer it. You just have to help Graham find a Snail Kite for me, okay?"

"That sounds like a deal," Lou says. "Once we find a boat it should be smooth sailing, no pun intended."

"Oh yeah! We went to the marsh, Mom. We met a couple of other birders that seemed even more into it than you, which is impressive."

"Ooh, exciting," Mom says.

Lou lets go of my mom's hand as her phone buzzes. She pulls it from her pocket and quickly checks the new message. Her face turns pale, like she's suddenly become a ghost.

"Oh, looks like my dad's ready for me. It was nice meeting you, The Infamous Graham's Mom," Lou says abruptly. "See you around!"

Lou's shoes squeak on the shiny floor as she bolts out into the hallway.

"Weird," I say. "Hope her dad's fine."

Mom looks worried.

"Me too, G. Me too."

CLUB MEMBERS ONLY

YOU KNOW HOW SOMETIMES YOU MEET PEOPLE AND IT'S LIKE YOU HARDLY have to explain yourself to them? Like you're two people that have always been in the same club, but you're just meeting for the first time? That's sort of like what it's been between me and Lou.

If I had to name our club, it'd be the "Worst Case Scenario Club." We take in new members daily, and our motto is something like: "We wish you weren't a part of it!"

The problem is that membership never stops growing. More and more people get to see what it's like in our club, and all of us are always waiting for the other shoe to drop. For the worst to finally happen.

I think that's why I like stuff like lying about bird facts.

Making up ridiculous stuff to laugh about is the only thing that gets me by, some days.

And although I wouldn't wish club membership on my worst enemy, not even Nick, it is nice to have company.

SHIPSHAPE

"YOU GUYS NEED A BOAT, HUH?" MOM ASKS. "YOU'RE NOT BECOMING A pirate on me now, are you?"

I smile.

"You know it. I'm made for the pirate life. Ten months at sea. Mysterious scars. Getting scurvy. The whole deal."

Mom laughs, and it's good to hear. It's been a while. Nurse Robb comes into my mom's room while she's busting up.

"Well, this is a sight for sore eyes," he says, scrubbing his hands in the sink.

"We really do need a boat, though. I think it's our best chance at finding a Snail Kite, getting further into the marsh."

Mom looks out the window. The yellowish-orange sunlight is stretched across the room. I see Mom reach for her phone.

"Robb, I could have a small watercraft delivered to this hospital room, right?" she says to her nurse friend.

"Oh, no problem," he says with a sarcastic tone, pushing buttons on the heart-rate monitor next to my mom's bed. "Make sure to have it sent to my attention, just to avoid the confusion with all the other boat deliveries we keep receiving."

"Perfect," she says, picking up her phone. "Graham, do you like red or green better?"

She turns her phone toward me to show the pictures of two canoes.

"Are you serious right now?" I ask, my jaw dropping.

"I mean, I'm having it delivered to Dom's house, but otherwise, yes," Mom says.

"I vote green," says Robb.

"I agree. Green is better," Mom says.

She taps on her phone screen a few more times.

"Done," she says with a proud smile. "But I get to be the one to name it. I'll have to think of something good."

"I don't think 'It All Happens for a Reason' will fit on the side of a canoe," I joke.

"No, I'll have to think of something perfect," Mom says.

"Robbb with three b's," says the nurse with a quick laugh.

"Ha! Who knows?"

"Well, you'll have time," I say. "Won't it take like a week for that to come? The contest ends Saturday, and it's already Tuesday."

"This is America, baby," Mom says with a wild look in her eye. "You want a canoe? It'll be in Dom's garage in less than twenty-four hours."

WELL, THAT'S NEW

YOU KNOW HOW SOMETIMES THINGS OR PLACES HAVE A NEW SMELL TO them?

Like when you get a new shirt, or a new comforter for your bed, and it always smells like the store you plucked it from?

Luckily, we don't have that problem in My Waiting Room, because nothing is ever new.

Do you want to know why I know that the HVAC vent kicks on every seventeen minutes? Or why the bathrooms get closed for an hourly, mysterious "cleaning" that never seems to take place? Every magazine in here is from last March and never fails to give you papercuts.

But lately something has been different in here. Really different.

There are still the two doors, which never change, but today I noticed another door. A new door. And now I'm standing in front of it. And through a circular window in the door, I can see Lou, who's telling me to open it. I do, and follow her along a mossy pathway away from waiting rooms and out of the doors of the hospital.

Outside, there are birds. And jokes. And adventures. And somebody else that knows how I feel.

And it feels good to leave My Waiting Room, even just for a little bit.

I'LL BE

Do not come here! Go help Dom or have fun with Lou or something! This is a direct order. ☺

I'm sitting at the kitchen counter, reading this message from my mom while quickly finishing off a chocolate doughnut. I texted Lou to see if she wanted to go birding on foot while we wait for our canoe today, but I haven't heard back.

"You comin' with today, DaVinci?" Dom asks me, filling his giant silver mug with coffee. "They say Wednesday is Italian for 'the day of painting for Dom.'"

"Why not? Will I actually get to paint today?"

"Let's hit the road and find out, bud. Time is money," he says. He turns toward Nick's room and shouts, "Have a good day, son! See you later!"

I forgo my backpack for today and follow Dom outside, grabbing my seat in the passenger side of the Blue Beast. It smells normal, which is to say it smells like old leather and sweat and stale energy drinks from yesteryear.

Dom finishes loading up the van and slams the back door shut. As he gets in the car behind the steering wheel, though, I hear the back side door open behind me.

"Huh?"

I turn around and watch as Nick hops into the backseat, slamming the door shut behind him before scooting down the bench seat. He's wearing a light-blue Dom and Son T-shirt.

"You feelin' okay? Need a lift somewhere?" Dom asks while looking in the rearview mirror, perplexed.

"I, uh, think I'm gonna join you today. Or whatever." Nick says.

"Want the front seat?" I offer.

"I'm fine," he says as he buckles his seatbelt. He puts his left elbow on the edge of the window and nervously taps his fingers on the glass.

"Well, I'll be," Dom says. "Let's go."

The morning is overcast and the sky is full of dark and moody clouds. Dom is silently sipping his coffee while driving the Blue Beast, and I keep looking out the passenger window as we cruise alongside marshy channels. Tiny bugs splatter on our slightly cracked windshield as we rumble down what seems like a lesser-traveled back road. Densely packed wilderness is on either side of us.

We reach an intersection with a flashing yellow light and take a left turn. I'm reminded how quickly everything turns from swampy to swanky. The scenery of overgrown bushes and weeds has left, and within seconds I'm now looking out at green lawns and trucks unloading landscaping equipment. I begin to recognize the neighborhood, and soon enough we're turning past the sign for Peerless Pines. I look at Nick in the back seat from the corner of my eye.

"You know we could try and drop by your mom's house, if you'd like," Dom says, looking at his son in the rearview mirror.

Nick doesn't reply and keeps looking left as his mom's house appears on the opposite side of the street. It's like he's refusing to look at his mom's place.

I peer through the slats of the white picket fence again. There are toys strewn across the yard, but once again nobody's outside.

"Maybe later," Dom says in a low tone.

"No thanks," Nick finally answers, slouching a bit.

Dom says nothing else as we continue into the neighborhood and finally reach the jobsite. We all hop out and start to unload cans of paint and new drop cloths from the van, but I can't help but feel something isn't quite right.

AMAZING GRAYS

I THINK I UNDERSTAND WHAT VAN GOGH OR FRIDA KAHLO MUST'VE FELT when they first picked up the tool of their trade. The rush of adrenaline. The opportunity a single paintbrush holds. The ten dollars an hour it will keep providing all summer. I finally get it, because today I am actually a painter. And sure, it's only the edges of each wall and mostly due to Dom's crew being gone on another job, but at least it's a start.

"Hey, do you think you could help me for a second?" Nick says from the doorway behind me. He's been working in a different room, and I'm honestly sort of surprised to hear his voice. He hasn't said a word all day.

"Sure," I say, setting my paintbrush down.

I follow Nick down the hallway, our shoes covered with little white booties so we don't ruin any of the new flooring. He takes a few steps into a room and I lean my head in.

"Okay, well, is this—"

"Wow! Purple. Very, very purple," I say, stepping in to look at the paint covering half the walls.

"I was afraid of that," Nick mumbles. "I guess I snagged the wrong paint. My dad's gonna be upset."

"It's fine. We can fix it. Nothing's broken or anything," I say. "We'll cover it with primer and start again. I have the blue paint in my room. I'll bring it over."

I go back and get the metal bucket of paint I've been using all day. I take it into Nick's purplish room and open the lid. I stir it with one of the thin wooden sticks that cover the floor of Dom's van.

"How's your mom doing?" Nick asks, rolling the white primer over any dried purple paint.

"Fine, I guess," I answer as I finish stirring. I think about asking him the same question but instead just pour the blue paint into a couple of plastic containers. We start going over the parts of the wall that are now purple, staying silent for a long stretch.

"Thanks for helping me out with this, or whatever," Nick mumbles, breaking the silence.

"No worries," I say. "Just remind me to never let you dye my hair."

"You're hilarious," Nick says, his face speckled with paint drops.

He seems a bit more relaxed than he was in the van ride over here.

"So, like, purple looks blue to you then?"

"I guess so," Nick says.

"Is it like that for all colors? Like, is some stuff invisible?"

"No, come on," Nick says, cracking a little smile. "It all looks normal to me, it's that everybody else sees it differently."

I nod.

"You know what? I think I kind of understand that," I say as we keep painting for a few quiet minutes.

It's relaxing and kind of therapeutic, painting a wall over and over. I try to only focus on keeping smooth brush strokes, like Dom instructed, but other than that you can't really overthink it or worry. You just . . . paint.

"You don't have to talk about it if you don't want to, but any reason you don't want to see your mom? I mean, she's your mom, right?" I ask, not taking my focus away from the wall.

Nick keeps working, choosing not to respond.

"Like, I've never even seen her. I've seen your best friends, for sure, but not many other people . . ." I say. I figure maybe a little button pushing might get a reply.

"They're not my best friends," he finally blurts out.

"Oh? It kind of seems like it."

Nick shoots me an annoyed look. "I barely even like those guys anyways. My parents are trying to make me go to their same private school. They live in this crummy neighborhood, too."

"And so you're coming here to see them instead of her? It sounds like you're avoiding your mom because . . . I don't really know why."

Nick puts his paint container down on the ground, laying his brush on top of its edge.

"You don't understand," he says.

"I don't know, man, I think I might," I answer. "I'm worried about losing my mom all the time. I get it. It's hard to think about what would happen if she wasn't around."

From downstairs I can hear Dom's stereo blasting some song as he whistles along.

"But my mom is doing it on purpose," Nick says, irritated. "So that's exactly why you don't get it."

"I mean, that's only how—"

"No," Nick says, cutting me off. "She's busy with her new life and her new kids that are screaming all the time."

I pause, hearing Dom's whistle echo through the empty hallways once more.

"The day you guys showed up was the twins' first birthday party," Nick says. "My dad was there the whole time and even built a little slide as a gift and everything. He never cares about what I think."

This reminds me of something I've heard of once before—a nurse described something like that as having a "do-over family." When somebody leaves what they've got and tries to make the family they'd always seen in their minds.

Is that what this is?

"If the twins weren't around, would you want to see your mom?"

"I don't even care. She's decided what's important to her," Nick says, looking out one of the big windows. "And I'm the kid that she doesn't want."

I remember that first night in Sugarland, where Nick said he couldn't imagine if his mom died. Which means, deep down he loves her.

My annoyance with Nick is starting to be replaced with something like sympathy. I mean, not having a parent is tough. But having a parent that doesn't want you . . . well, that's almost worse.

A PROPER BURIAL

NICK AND I BOTH JUMP AS WE HEAR A LOUD THWANG! FROM THE BIG window on the other side of the room. I walk toward it.

"What was that?" Nick asks. "It was loud."

I press my forehead against the glass and look down. Below me is a bird, its neck bent at an unnatural angle.

"Oh no," I whisper. "It must've flown into the window."

I look for a few more seconds and I can tell the bird isn't moving. I head to find Dom, who's painting the front door a deep red. On the way through the kitchen, I snag a pair of blue rubber gloves, normally used for working with chemicals.

"Dom, I think a bird flew into one of those picture windows," I say to him. "It looks like it might've died."

"Let's go take a look," Dom answers.

Nick and I follow him around the side of the house, stepping on decorative stones that have been planted in the yard. Dom has a sort of bowlegged walk, like a cowboy who's been riding a horse from Yuma all day.

We get to the bird and Dom surveys the situation.

"Welp, unfortunately it doesn't look like it made it, DaVinci. Sometimes they can be stunned and unconscious for a few hours and be revived, but this one is definitely not breathing. Broken neck. These owners need to get some of that reflective tape that helps birds see the glass." Dom shakes his head. "It's a Palm Warbler. Beautiful birds. A family lived under my porch one winter."

The wind picks up and I watch the fluffy feathers of the bird softly move in the breeze. It's mostly brown in color, but I can see some bright-yellow feathers around its tail and belly.

"How's about I go get something we can dig a hole with," Dom says, heading back toward the driveway. "We'll give it a proper burial."

I know it's only one tiny little bird, but it's sad to see it so lifeless.

"Bring it down toward the water, it'll be nice there," Dom hollers back.

I put the gloves on and gently pick up the bird, wishing it might suddenly fly away. It doesn't, though, and I start walking with its small, warm body in my hands. I carefully head toward the fence all the way in the back of the property.

"Why not right here, under this mahogany tree?" comes Dom's voice from behind me. He's caught up and is nearly next to me, pointing at a patch of fresh soil. In his hand is a small gardening trowel.

"That looks fine to me," I say. Dom digs a hole about a foot down with only a few fast scoops. I kneel down on my right knee and lower the bird into its final resting place. Dom pushes the dark soil on top, filling in the deep hole.

"Want to say any final words?" Dom asks, taking off his hat. He smooths his paint-covered hair back.

"Um. Let me think," I say, caught by surprise.

"Fair enough, but the ten bucks an hour doesn't apply to bird funerals," Dom says as he clasps his hands behind his back.

I begin to think about how this bird died, how it thought it was headed into several thousand square feet of paradise. But instead, in an instant, everything changed.

"What if it doesn't all happen for a reason? What if we're all trying to get by, and one day we hit a window?" I say, staring at the ground. "What then?"

I stay quiet for a second and listen to the birds overhead, unaware and happily chirping their favorite birdsongs.

"Well, as far as funerals go that was pretty dark, DaVinci. But to each his own," Dom says, flopping his hat back on and producing yet another toothpick. "Now let's head up, there's lots more to do."

MESSAGE

Since Dom asked Nick to ride up front on the way home, I'm on the back bench seat holding onto the handle attached to the ceiling. Really, though, my eyes are closed and I'm in my canoe. Or at least what I hope it might look and feel like. It's big and sturdy, and it's like every movement is magnified. I'm floating and bouncing and defying gravity—but that might also be the broken springs in the Blue Beast.

For some reason, Nick is with me in my boat, too. He's in the front, facing forward, the tips of his hair slightly purple. I feel like, I don't know, I maybe see him a little differently now that we got to talk. He's not really an awful person, just a little sad. Nobody seems to understand him.

Splash!

Waves come from up ahead of us and rock the canoe. There's something thrashing in the water, and it seems big—ancient alligator big. I look down at the water and only see tons of seaweed and brownish murky water. The water starts flowing forward and we gradually move with it on a little current, like a tide pulling us in.

I put my paddle in the water to steer but don't have to do much more than that. We start to pick up speed and soon we're moving fast. Then it feels like we're moving too fast, as we bash into fallen trees and huge rocks. That's when I see it. Where the splashing is coming from. The Fossil. Its gator head is bigger than a FedEx truck, and it has red glowing eyes. Its teeth are sharp . . . and there's a lot of them.

Grrr.

It opens its prehistoric, gnarled jaws. The water around us begins to rush in, heading toward the black abyss of the giant gator's mouth. It's a huge black hole. We're heading straight for it.

I yell to Nick to spin the canoe around and we dig hard, trying to fight the current sweeping us back. I paddle and paddle but it's no use. The boat goes sideways and Nick is getting closer and closer to the Fossil's mouth. Above us is a thick tree branch. I reach up and grab it with both hands. I hold on tight, wedging my feet under my canoe seat, but the current is pulling us back.

As I release my left hand and think of letting go, a large gray bird with orange feet flies down and perches on the tree next to me. It's the Snail Kite. Its chirp is loud and kind of funky, like the sound your cheek makes when you eat something sour.

It looks right at me until I put my hand back on the tree. It's telling me to hold on. To keep holding on. So I do, until it squawks once more and flies away.

Ka-chunk!

My eyes snap open as Dom's van winds across another poorly maintained back road.

I look back out the window as we cruise past groves of citrus trees. My heart is beating wildly. Even though it wasn't real—the canoe, the alligator, the Snail Kite—it felt real. My pulse pounds. It's not the scary monster gator that my brain is fixated on—it's the Snail Kite. If birds are here to send messages, I wonder what it is telling me.

THE EAGLE HAS LANDED

"Gotta say, y'all did a good job today. Real good job," Dom says.

We're nearly home, and I can tell Dom is happy. Not only did we finish work early, but the radio is turned up louder than usual and he's playing the drum parts to each song on the steering wheel.

"You've got a real eye for detail there, fella," Dom says to Nick. "Making us all look bad in comparison."

He playfully whacks Nick on the knee as we come to the familiar flashing-yellow-light intersection.

"Thanks," he says, staring out the passenger side window. The clock in the van says it's just after 2 p.m.

"And nice work on the trim today, DaVinci. You'll be painting a Mona Lisa in a month at this rate," Dom adds.

We turn at the light and keep heading toward home. The closer we get, the more I'm aware that our neighborhood doesn't have fancy cars or landscapers. It has gravel driveways and twisted old trees. But you know what? I kind of prefer it that way.

"Well, look at that," Dom says as we round a turn near the house. Down the driveway, in front of the garage door is a huge box.

"No way, even less than twenty-four hours!" I exclaim from the backseat. I'm leaning forward in between Nick and Dom.

"What is that thing?" Nick questions. Dom parks the van and I exit with an explosive run out of the back door.

"My canoe! Man, this is awesome! I wanna take it out right away." I start ripping at the packaging, trying to pry open the box without scissors. It's unwieldy and awkward, but before long, I'm able to rip through the cardboard and tape.

I grab my phone and furiously type out a text to Lou:

Wahoo, canoe! It's here! Wanna take it for a spin?

"Hold on there now, DaVinci," says Dom. "You have to take Dom's Boat Safety Course before I can, in good conscience, send you out into that mess."

I gape at him. "What do I have to do to complete Dom's Boat Safety?"

Honk! Honk!

I turn around to see a white SUV pulling down the driveway.

"Hey there, friends!" says the woman driving. She seems about my mom's age and is waving her hand energetically while the bracelets on her wrist clang together. She's wearing red sunglasses and a bright green athletic long-sleeve shirt. Her curly dark hair is pulled up in a ponytail. The stereo is bumping.

"Hey there, Angie," Dom says with a warm smile. He walks up to her and the two start to chat as the vehicle stops. The back two doors open and I watch as DJ and Zane spill out from either side of the SUV, each again wearing polo shirts and supremely unscuffed sneakers. Nick's friends walk up next to my canoe and start to inspect the semishredded box holding it.

"Have fun boys, and be good," she says.

"Of course, we will," says DJ.

"You've got some upstanding kids. I mean that," Dom says. "They say *please* and *thank you*. They even eat food at an actual table. Perfect gentlemen that could teach Nick a thing or two."

I look at Nick, who rolls his eyes. Zane and DJ keep their sheepish, faux-humble smirks glued to their faces. I wonder if they teach that at rich-kid school.

DJ and Zane's mom waves. "My appointment won't be long at all. It's so nice you're this close to the hospital, I appreciate being able to drop the guys off. Be right back."

Dom starts heading through the open garage door as the SUV heads back down the tree-lined driveway. "Meet me down at the dock in thirty, DaVinci," he says. "Invite your friend, too, if she's using the canoe. And wear a swimsuit. You will be in the splash zone."

Once Dom is gone, Zane and DJ immediately start inspecting the box as though it's their package. Once DJ sees the photo on the side of the box, he scoffs. "This thing doesn't even have a motor? Dude, it's worthless. You should send it back."

"Not having a motor is kind of the point of it," I say, finishing up ripping the clear wrapping tape.

"Whatever. Nick you ready? If we have to be stuck over here, let's go look for cash," DJ says. "And get away from Mr. Canoe Bird Guy over here. Like he's some pathetic superhero."

"Yeah," Nick says with a fake laugh. "The infamous Bird Boy."

I try not to cringe. It's like Nick has changed personalities in the span of a van ride.

"Ha! I like that. Have fun with your hunk of junk, Bird Boy," DJ calls as the three of them cut through the garage toward the backyard. As Nick leaves the back door of the garage, I feel him look back, but I've already turned and walked away.

DOM'S WATER SAFETY

"WHERE'S YOUR FRIEND, DAVINCI? SHOULD WE GET STARTED?" SAYS DOM
from atop the wooden dock behind his house. He's wearing a tattered
orange life jacket and faded swimwear.

"I let her know to meet me here, but I haven't heard from her
yet," I reply. I stare down at my phone again, hoping for an update.

"I'll get started and you can bring her up to speed," Dom says,
leaning on a canoe oar. "Now let me hop in here and show you how
it's done."

Dom bends down and takes a long step into the boat. It starts
wobbling, and Dom throws his arms around wildly to keep his balance. He finally sits on the wooden seat at the back of the canoe.

"Careful, I hear there's gators!" comes Lou's voice from the trail
leading toward us. When I get a view of her, I see she's wearing her
birding outfit, the hat Loretta gave her, and a huge goofy smile.

"I was beginning to think you weren't coming," I say, shielding my eyes from the sun.

"And miss this? Never," Lou replies.

She steps onto the wooden dock and gives me a playful nudge with her elbow.

"That's a good-looking canoe. Green was the perfect choice," she says. "Your mom is amazing."

"Okay, Lewis and Clark, if you're going to be one with nature, I've got to share my safety ways with you guys."

Dom has a canoe paddle dipped in the water, which is keeping him facing us.

"First thing's first, everybody wears a life jacket at all times. No exceptions," Dom says, holding up one finger. He holds up another. "The second rule is: always have a buddy. And if you're buddy's not me, you both have to let me know where you're headed and when you'll be back."

"That sounds fair," I say.

"More smart than fair. This is serious stuff. Now moving on," Dom explains as he wraps his left hand around the top of the paddle and grabs halfway down with his right. "When you paddle, you're going to want to hold it like so."

He dips his paddle into the water. A tiny school of fish nibbles at the top of the greenish water and then darts away.

"This is what we call a 'J stroke,' and that's *J* as in Jethro Tull Wrongfully Received a Hard Rock Grammy," Dom says.

"What?" Lou and I say in unison.

"It means you dip your paddle in the shape of the letter, like so."

Dom pulls the paddle toward him and a rush of bubbles swirl behind.

"Now whoever's in the back, you'll steer. You dip your paddle in on either side like this."

The canoe begins to veer right and eventually winds up in a patch of lily pads.

"Definitely works better with two people in the canoe. Graham, why don't you hop in front and try it with me. It'll be your first voyage."

Dom glides up next to the dock and I sit down on the edge, slithering my way into the wobbly canoe. I climb onto the seat in front. I like the feel of the part-plastic, part-wood bench and the buoyancy underneath me. It's almost like I'm floating, which, well *technically* I am. Lou hands me my paddle and we coast out beyond the lily pads and hyacinth. I still can't believe my mom got this canoe for me.

"Third rule: don't go past the third canal bridge. Gators and things like to sleep and hide during the day, but that'll put you out into the Salvato Marsh. I'd say stay closer than that until you're ready."

Lou gives me a silent look as if to say, "We'll see about that."

"And the fourth safety rule is to always be prepared. Keep your head on a swivel," Dom says. We stop moving forward and I look behind me to see what Dom's doing now. He's holding his paddle up over his head with two hands. "You'll never know when you might . . . capsize."

Dom throws his body to the right and the canoe rolls and begins to fill with water. Before I can lean the other way to balance out the weight, it completely turns over, tossing me headlong into the swamp.

"Ah!" I shout before water fills my nose and mouth. The moment I'm fully submerged is a strange one. Though I'm panicking, my body is moving in slow motion. It's almost peaceful. I come up under the canoe, breathing the bubble of trapped air inside. Dom swims under to join me.

"Ooowee! Now we're swimming! Don't it make you feel alive!?" Dom hoots. His voice echoes in the hollow chamber.

I sneeze and shake my head from side to side. I think a gallon of river water just shot up my nose.

"Yegh, rightth. Alivfth."

"And if you ever see a gator, my man, just stay cool," Dom says. "No gettin' in the water, no sudden moves. They'll leave you alone if you leave them alone. *Hakuna matata*, or whatever the kids say these days."

Dom ducks back out from under the canoe, and I sit there alone for another second, my breath echoing off the canoe. The water is giving everything a creepy green ambient light, and as I look down I see a shadow under the canoe. For a second, it looks like a scaly prehistoric tail.

But as a faded Nike swoosh comes into view I exhale. It's just Dom's leg.

First Trip

"Okay, are you steering, or am I?" Lou asks from the seat opposite me. "I get the feeling I'll be better at paddling."

"What makes you say that?!"

"You've got puny landlocked Buffalo arms."

I look at my forearms and am reminded that they are still splattered with paint from the workday.

"Graham's Bird Fact: buffalo had wings until 2008."

Lou chuckles as her phone dings with a few messages. She opens it and scrolls through, pausing to look for a minute. I glance at my phone, too. It's almost 4 p.m.

"Actually, how about I steer," Lou says as she lazily drags her paddle in the water to her right side. She's peering over her sunglasses at her phone.

"Suit yourself," I say.

I spin around and face forward, out over the front of the canoe. I felt a little uneasy at first, but I'm starting to get the hang of trying to keep our balance on top of the water. I dig my paddle in and alternate from side to side, doing my best to make the shape of a *J*. Today is overcast and humid and you can hardly see the sun through the clouds.

"I was thinking about something the other day," I say. "I realized you and me are in 'The Worst Case Scenario Club.'"

Lou doesn't say anything.

"You know how clubs are usually, like, exclusive? Or, like, invite only? Well, ours is a club for people with the worst luck ever. The only requirement for membership is that your life is constantly bad news."

I keep splashing forward but crane my neck to look back at Lou. She stays quiet for a few more moments.

"I don't know if I agree," she says, resting her paddle across her knees.

"But we see life differently. How hard it is."

"Maybe," Lou replies. "I don't know, though. Sometimes I think we're the lucky ones. We see what's really important in life, right?"

I spin back to face Lou.

"With homeschool I don't have too many classmates, you know? But last year I had this friend Becca who lived down the street. We did everything together, and she was the only person I've met that ever cared to know everything there is about manatees with me."

"What happened?" I ask.

"Boys. Being popular. She kind of became annoyingly obsessed with it all, so when I started going through health stuff with my dad, she magically never wanted to hang out again. She lives five houses down and we don't even talk anymore."

I keep looking at her, unsure what to say. But I know the feeling of never hearing from people again.

"I'd rather know what really matters to me now than spend an entire lifetime trying to figure it out," Lou says, looking up at the moss-covered tree branches overhead. "So, for me, that's a club I'd rather be in."

"Huh. Guess I never thought of it that way. I'm really sorry about your friend."

Lou shrugs.

I spin back around and start to paddle again. We're nearly to the spot we made it to with Nick, which means the Salvato Marsh should be close. It doesn't feel like Lou is paddling or steering, though. We keep drifting toward the banks on either side, our canoe scraping over green lily pads holding tiny white flowers.

As we glide toward land, I see a clearing through the reeds in the shallow water. It looks like a path has been worn down, with a lot of snapped reeds near packed-down dirt.

"I think they call these gator slides," I say. "There's a warning in those maps."

I study the ground for petrified alligator poop, but luckily don't see anything. We keep heading toward the clearing.

"Let's head to the left," I say to Lou.

I paddle a few times, but we stay on our same path toward the shore. "Lou?"

"Oh, sorry," she says, as I finally hear her paddle break the water. Something is off with her.

"Want to head back?" I ask.

"Yeah, I think so."

I don't push it any further and start turning us around.

"Wait! Do you see that?" Lou says. She's holding her arm out and pointing at the water.

"What is it?"

I gaze up at the sky, hoping to see our contest-winning bird above us, but I only see fast-moving clouds in the blue sky.

"Not up there, silly. Floating there on the top of the water, you see it?"

I look down and finally see what Lou is talking about: a gray-ish-blue feather!

"Is that from a Snail Kite, do you think?" I ask.

"It could be," Lou answers. "Right?"

I stretch out my arm and grab it, tucking it into a crevice on my wooden bench. My eyes dart around at the thick trees all around us. A Snail Kite has to be in here somewhere.

"We're getting closer to finding it, I can feel it!" I say to Lou, who's looking through the zoom lens on her dad's camera.

"Ready to get our winning photo!"

I'm getting excited. We lift our paddles and float in the quiet for another minute, the air soon filling with the shrieks of grasshoppers and frogs. But after a few minutes, I hear the rumbling of distant thunder. The air is super-humid. A late afternoon storm is coming. I look over at Lou, whose smile fades as she examines the dark clouds moving in above.

"Should we head back?" I ask Lou.

She sighs and nods. "Yeah, probably."

I feel my shoulder muscles burning as I spin our canoe around, making sure to avoid branches and fallen trees jutting up from the water. I'm still thinking about the feather I have tucked between the wood planks of my seat, a talisman that our Snail Kite is near.

Lou remains quiet as we canoe back. I can't tell if it's because she's sad or just tired from all the paddling. I wonder if she's still thinking about the friend who ditched her.

"Where should we stash the boat?" she finally asks as we get closer to the dock with Nick's boat. "I don't trust Nick and his friends."

"Good point."

Just before we get to the dock, I spot a big grouping of thorny bushes.

"We could probably hide it over there," I say. "Since it's green, it should blend in pretty well."

"Perfect."

We try to lean a bunch of dead branches over the canoe in our best efforts to camouflage it. By the time we're done, and after more than a few scratches and a lot of sweat, the canoe is only visible if you really know where to look.

"That'll do, I think," Lou says surveying our work with her hands on her hips.

We follow the trail back to the house. We walk faster as fat rain-drops start bouncing off leaves next to us. A light rain has started by the time we make it back to the yard, where we're greeted by Dom stepping out of the glass sliding door. He's got his phone pressed to his ear and is waving to us to hurry.

"What's up?" I ask, a little winded after jogging the length of Dom's long backyard. "Bad storm on the way?"

"Graham, we've got to go to the hospital. Your mom has some news."

To the Top

WE GET TO MY MOM'S ROOM, ONLY IT'S NOT MY MOM'S ROOM, AT LEAST it's not the one she's been in for the last week or so. We've been following signs pointing us toward the ICU, which I know from experience stands for Intensive Care Unit. The place where the sickest patients go.

"There you are!" Mom says with enthusiasm. A handful of new nurses are swarming around her, setting up rows of screens and monitors next to my mom's bed.

"What's the news?" I ask her, crammed into the tiny room with Lou. Dom's waiting in the hallway. I can see him through the walls that are made of glass, put there so attending nurses can keep an eye on patients that aren't doing well.

"You're not even going to try to guess?" Mom says, disappointed for ruining her fun.

"You're going to Disney World?" Lou jokes.

"You guys," Mom says, rolling her eyes. "The list! I'm a 1!"

One is what we've been waiting for. The top of the list. The tippy top.

"Wait, did you move up?" Lou says. "That's great news!"

"Thank you, Lou! I'd agree. But there's a lot that has to go right for us to even have a chance at our miracle."

"But you're so close!" Lou says.

"Well, then, I'm camping out with you till it comes!" I tell Mom.

"Graham, you can't."

"This is what we've waited for forever, and I need to make sure I'm here when it's time. It could be any day—it could be tonight!"

"I understand, I really do, honey. But the only seat in here is for a nurse right now," she explains.

"So, I'll bring in another chair!"

Mom smirks.

"I don't need to be babied, I can handle this," I say. "There's absolutely no way I'm leaving if you're next on the list, though."

"I'd never baby you. Promise," she says. "It could take weeks, months even, for the right heart to become available."

I look around the room at all the intimidating machines. They seem mysterious and menacing.

"You're going to be in here for months?"

"I hope not," she says emphatically. "We have to remember that this is a good thing! We're close! It's always darkest before dawn."

"Did you pick up a new saying in here?" I say.

"That one was your father's, believe it or not."

She's never mentioned that before. It seems like I'm learning all sorts of new things about my dad here in Sugarland.

"What am I supposed to do while you're in here, then?" I ask.

"Find the Snail Kite for us, G. For me. Do it as a 'Heart Day' present. If you can find our island, I just know you're going to find it. Maybe it'll even have a message for me."

Mom winks and squeezes my hand with hers. It's so thin and weak I hardly recognize it. While she says being in here is good news, I can't help but have a bad feeling in the pit of my stomach.

"No visitors allowed right now, sorry, guys," says a busy nurse who's shuffling into the room, helping my mom get set up. I hug my mom tight and let her know I'll see her tomorrow, then follow Lou into the hallway.

"You heard your mom. We've got a bird to find. Let's get out of here," Lou says, walking briskly toward the elevator. "I hate the ICU."

WORST OF THE WORST

EVEN THOUGH I'M EXCITED THAT MY MOM IS TOP OF THE LIST, AS I LOOK at the sad, tired faces of everyone in the hallway a new realization hits me. In hospitals there are a million abbreviations for everything. Some days you have to get an EKG, followed by a CT scan, then all topped off with an invigorating MRI. But going to the ICU, the Intensive Care Unit, is never something you want to hear.

My mom was in one once before, in Seattle. She was rushed into the emergency room and spent a day in there. You're basically in a room with glass walls, where a team of nurses and doctors are constantly monitoring you. It's intense.

And now, the more I think about it, I know what my mom going in there means. My mom moved up the list because her heart is getting worse. Like, bad. When you're at the top of the list, then that means you're the worst of the worst. We're running out of time.

YEAR OF OUR FJORD

"Have you ever been to Norway?" Lou asks me on the pathway to the dock behind Dom's house. Even though I felt like doing nothing, she convinced me that going birding would take my mind off things. I hope she's right. The evening air is sticky and the sun is slowly beginning to set. It's almost 7 p.m. Wednesday, which means we basically have seventy-two hours left in the contest.

"Do I look like a guy that's been to Norway? I'm not even sure where that is."

"It's in northern Europe, almost to the Arctic Circle. The national bird is a Dipper," Lou says. My canoe paddle bangs on a few branches hanging over the path.

"Why are you suddenly interested in that?"

"I don't know. I was reading about fjords and I realized I've never seen one before. Seems like something you should see once in your life, right?"

"Fjords? Is that a car that runs on fish?"

"Your jokes are the worst. Like, worse than Gary's. Really awful," Lou grumbles. "But seriously, don't you want to go out and explore everything there is to explore? Isn't there anywhere you want to visit?"

I try to think, but I can't really come up with anything.

"Most times when we travel it's just to get to the next hospital, so I don't really have a choice in it," I finally answer.

"You're telling me there's not one place in the world you want to see in your life?"

"Umm . . ."

Lou stops on the path, leaning on her canoe paddle.

"Okay, right now, at this moment, let's say you can go anywhere in the world. Where do you go?"

"Swansen's?"

"You're hopeless, Graham Dodds."

Lou and I make it to Nick's dock and walk past his boat, searching for our camouflaged canoe.

"There it is," I say, finally spotting the green paint.

Seeing a canoe of our very own fills me with a sense of hope that we have a chance at spotting the bird today. I'm worried any minute we might see they've announced the winners on the website (I've been checking).

As we inch closer to our boat, though, I can tell something is different than how we left it. The branches hiding it have been moved.

"What is this?!" Lou says.

The words *BIRD BOY* are scrawled onto the side in sloppy black ink, and there is an enormous hole. A carved-out chunk almost big enough for a golf ball to pass through.

"It's ruined," I say, tracing my fingertips over the letters scribbled onto the heavy plastic. "This will sink right away, there's no way we can take this out."

I feel something boiling inside of me, red-hot and angry. I wind up and kick the side of the canoe.

Why does nothing in my life ever go my way? I feel all at once enraged and deflated. I look over at Lou. She's just staring out at the water with eyes that seem empty. I sit on top of the canoe and put my head between my knees.

I know exactly who put this hole in our canoe, and a new wave of anger hits me. I've never hated anyone before. But this—*this*—must be what it feels like.

"I'm just sick of feeling stuck all the time, you know?" I say to the ground. "Like nothing gets to be normal or easy for me. Even when I try to do something I wind up with a freaking hole in my boat. I'm stuck with bad luck forever."

I look back up at Lou and can tell she's got tears in her eyes.

"Lou?"

"If you want life to be normal and easy and full of only good luck, I've got some bad news for you, Graham," Lou says, wiping her eyes with the back of her hand.

She says nothing more and starts back toward the house.

"Hey, wait up!" I shout, trying to catch up to Lou. I double-time it, but she's moving too fast. By the time I get to the garage, her bike is already gone.

MOVIN' OUT (GRAHAM'S SONG)

I HAVE NEVER ENJOYED MOVING.

I don't know if anybody ever does, though. It's not that it's annoying merely packing all your stuff up, but it's having to say goodbye to people and places that makes it hard. Buffalo was the first place I played for the soccer team, and it was hard to say goodbye to everybody.

But when you're moving out of a room you're sharing with the careless person that helped drill a hole in your boat? In that case, moving can be kind of fun.

After finding my ruined canoe, I've spent my whole Thursday alone, taking all my stuff from Nick's room and piling it in the corner of my new residence. It's where my mom was staying before she had to be admitted into the hospital. If she still might be gone for a few months, I figure I can take up residence here until she gets back. Or we leave. Or both.

For now, though, I plan to stay put in this room. Nothing else can go wrong if I do nothing.

FRIDAY

TODAY IS ONE OF THOSE DAYS WHERE IT SEEMS LIKE NOBODY WANTS TO TALK to you, you know? Like the world has flipped over the OPEN sign to CLOSED and everything is shut down. Since doctors have been doing test after test the past few days, I haven't been allowed to see my mom at all. And Lou hasn't replied to a text or call since Wednesday.

Meanwhile I'm stuck waiting around hospital lobbies once again, trying my best to avoid any possible Bad Day vibes.

For the last ten minutes I've been staring at a watercolor painting of the ocean that's stuck to one of the walls in the ICU waiting area. In it there are sets of waves building in the blue water, with a few crashing on the sandy shore in white foamy curls.

For some reason I'm reminded of a few years ago, when a teacher in Seattle was teaching everybody about riptides and currents. She talked about how there's something called an undercurrent. It's whenever a river or body of water looks like it's flowing one way on the surface, but underneath there's a current going in another direction. It's super-dangerous. Undercurrents can pull you under, never to see the surface again. After flipping the boat with Dom, I think I get it.

Most days it's as if my stomach and heart are in their own undercurrent of dread—expecting the worst no matter what life seems to be like on the surface. Something always seems to be there, trying to pull me under and away.

I wonder if Lou ever gets that with her dad. If she feels the same things, too. Maybe that's why I haven't heard from her. I hope she isn't sucked under for good.

HOLE IN YOUR BUCKET

"You up, DaVinci?" says Dom's voice.

I slowly open my eyes. "I am now."

I scratch my head and sit up, still half-asleep. I'm home in my new room. Out the window next to my bed the sun is starting to set behind cotton candy clouds. After coming back from the hospital, I must have dozed off.

Dom leans in the doorway and takes a bite from a green apple.

"I was down by the water and noticed you've got a hole in your watercraft," Dom says. "Throw your swimming trunks on, man. Let's go take care of it." He doesn't remark on my change of scenery.

"It doesn't matter, I can't really use a canoe by myself anyways," I say.

I look at my phone and see I still haven't heard from Lou at all, not even a text since she ran off. I think she's given up on the contest. The deadline for spotting a Snail Kite is tomorrow, and, honestly, thinking about it makes me depressed. A few days ago, I was certain we were going to find this bird and everything was going to work out fine. Now it just seems pointless.

"Can we do it tomorrow?" I groan.

"Who knows? You have to live life when you can," Dom says. "Plus I've got to help my friend Dennis empty a few port-a-potties tomorrow before heading on vacation. Come on, let's go."

SUGARLAND MOSS

"Boy, somebody really did a number on this thing. Who would do something like this?" Dom says, sizing up the magnitude of the hole in the canoe.

I know exactly who, but I don't feel like being a snitch. What's the point anyways? The contest is now theirs to win. I was able to wash off the writing with water, but the canoe crater remains.

"Do you think we can fix it?"

"Luckily whoever did this underestimated the sheer amount of sprayable liquid rubber I purchased off one of those "As-Seen-On-TV" ads. We'll be good in no time," Dom says. "You can fix whatever you set your mind to, DaVinci. Sometimes life is nothin' but leaky boats that you have to patch. You do your best and keep things moving."

Dom shakes up a white canister and sprays a yellow foam in the chiseled-out chunk of the boat.

"Now, just don't breathe that in and give it fifteen minutes to dry and we're golden," Dom says, covering his mouth with his arm. "Actually, it's a nice night for a cruise. Pink sky at night, sailor's delight. Pink sky at morning, sailors take warning."

Dom goes over to Nick's boat and starts it up.

Burububububurb.

"Get in. I promise I won't flip you over this time. Scout's honor," Dom says, holding his hand to his heart.

"Okay, fine."

I get in the boat and soon we're coasting over the greenish water. Insects are chirping all around us, and they all seem to get loud and then soft in unison.

With Dom guiding us, I can relax and look around. So far, I've seen five iguanas. A few of them were dangling their leathery tails off low-hanging tree branches.

"This is the third bridge coming up," Dom says. "You know this is where your dad and I used to come in high school."

"My mom said the same thing."

"Yeah, but he and I found it first. One summer we built an epic fire pit. We were moving rocks all day for a week, like a swamp Stonehenge."

I've been enjoying learning more about my dad. I guess I've never asked about him much.

"What do you remember most about my dad?"

Dom thinks for a second.

"He gave everybody a chance. Not everyone does that," Dom says. "And he never let people give up on their dreams, however silly they were. Heck, he's the one who suggested I start a painting business."

"Really?"

"Oh yeah. That's probably because I owed him three hundred bucks for wrecking his dad's car, though."

The tiny motor gets quiet as Dom eases off the gas.

"Were you guys always close friends, you and my dad?"

"I mean, he and I almost got into a fight the first time I met your mom."

"No way."

"Yes way. I'd figured that island was supposed to be our secret spot, but it soon became your parents' spot. They'd be out there all the time. Guess I just felt a little defensive of it."

I watch as the sun begins to set. It's another explosion of Sugarland colors, warm reds and yellows stretching across the sky. I snap a photo and remind myself to text it to Lou once I regain cell service. It's such beautiful scenery, it almost feels impossible that anything dangerous could exist out here.

"Have you ever heard of the Fossil?" I ask Dom, remembering my conversation with Gary about the colossal creature.

"Now I'm usually one for scary stories, but that Fossil's no joke. Not that you will, but if you ever see anything, try to be big and loud. Build a fire if you can," Dom says while surveying the trees next to us. "And another thing? It's pretty easy to get lost in here. I always look for Sugarland moss, you can only find it here and it always grows on the north side of the trees. Sometimes it helps you get your bearings."

I reach out and touch a spongy greenish-blue moss that's clinging to one side of a tree. It's soft and velvety, like nature's fuzzy pajamas.

Our boat drifts toward the center of the canal after Dom sends us away from the treeline with a push. He turns the tiny motor on once again and we begin heading back home to our dock.

"And before I forget to mention it, I'm going to go visit my brother in Sarasota tomorrow night. That way we can be up early Sunday for the boat races. We go every year, it's our tradition."

"Do I have to go?"

"No way man, this is my vacation. Nick's gonna have a sleepover with DJ and Zane, and I said you'd go with 'em."

My stomach drops.

"And by 'go with them,' you of course mean stay at the house and order Swansen's delivery?"

"C'mon, it'll be fun. Those guys are great, real stand-up fellas."

My stomach drops again. I'm too tired to try and put up a fight.

Dom eases up on the throttle and we slow down to the speed of a manatee.

"DaVinci, can I ask you a question about Nick?"

"I hear boarding school far away is nice," I nearly blurt, but Dom's tone of voice is telling me something is bothering him, though, so I clear my throat and speak up. "Sure, ask away."

He lets out a big breath and scratches the back of his head.

"I, uh, well . . . what do I do about Nick?" Dom says, his voice low and uncertain. "Ever since his mom remarried and had the twins, he hasn't been the same. The kids just turned one and I think he's only seen them once or twice. He said he won't visit because the twins scream too loud. But isn't that what babies do?"

I feel conflicted. While I don't feel like helping Nick after the hole in my boat, it's hard seeing Dom so serious and worried. We sit for a few seconds as a loose *V* of ducks quack overhead. Our boat feels like it's dancing on the water, gently bobbing over each tiny ripple.

Bzzzz.

A tiny cloud of mosquitoes begins to appear from the shadows. I slap one on as it lands next to my ear. I take the bug spray from the floor of the boat and blast myself with a cloud of it. I toss the tiny bottle to Dom and sigh.

"I think when he says the twins scream a bunch, I'm not so sure that's really the problem," I say to Dom.

He nods in agreement from his own cloud of bug spray.

"I think he feels, I don't know, forgotten. Like he's been replaced."

Dom is silent.

"I didn't really know about that. He's never mentioned it."

"I bet if you asked him about it, he'd tell you."

I glance out at the reflections on the water.

"Nick and I don't really *do* that—ask each other about that stuff," Dom says.

"Well, it's never too late to start. Who knows what might happen? I seem to remember someone telling me that you can fix anything if you put your mind to it."

"Hmmm, you know you're pretty wise, kid?" Dom says as the motor speeds up again.

My ears heat up. I turn to face forward again and look at my phone, hoping there might be a message from Lou. There's still no service, though, and she still hasn't responded all day. I put my phone away and look toward the setting sun.

"Thanks," I eventually say. "For taking me out and fixing my boat. And, well, for everything else."

"Don't mention it," Dom says as he revs the motor. "Now let's head home. Don't want to get caught out here in the dark."

SATURDAY

FOR SOME REASON, PRECISELY AT 4:44 A.M., MY EYES SNAP OPEN AND I'M wide awake. I can't seem to stop thinking about my mom, alone in the ICU. It's like part of me is there with her. I can almost feel an IV in my wrist. I start to look at my phone, but there are no new messages. I haven't heard from Lou since the boat incident, and the last message from my mom has so many misspellings I can tell her hands were shaking all over the place.

I don't know why I woke up. But it feels important.

It feels like something is wrong, but I don't know what.

All I know is that I won't be getting any more sleep tonight.

Sneaking Around

"OKAY, FOLLOW ME," SAYS ROBB AS HE WAVES ME INTO THE HALLWAY leading into the ICU. "I can't believe I'm doing this."

When I'd arrived at the hospital this morning, the doctors told me she was too critical for visitors. Apparently, they couldn't control her heart rate and she nearly had a heart attack early this morning. I found Robb and asked him for a favor. I needed to see my mom. He said he understood.

I follow him into the ICU, and I see life is up for grabs here. Nurses are rushing past me, and it seems like everywhere I look, there's some sort of emergency. I slip into my mom's little corner of the ICU.

"Mom?" I whisper.

She's asleep, so I sit down in the black plastic chair next to her. I move the journal out of my back pocket and put it on my lap. It's got a bend down the middle from being jammed in my back pocket and Swansen's grease spots on the back cover.

"This thing is a mess. We'll have to get you a new one when you're out of here," I say. "I may or may not have dropped a burger on it."

From her nose runs an oxygen tube, and various other wires are stuck across her shoulders. The tower of liquid IV medications looks scary.

I watch a screen that's monitoring her heart rate. It's sporadic and sometimes gets way too fast. There's no real rhythm.

"Oh," Robb says, pushing a few buttons on a machine. "She's a fighter, this one. Hanging in there."

I hold my mom's hand. There's no more pretending to be okay. Or suffering through it. She is not okay.

"I wish I knew what I'm supposed to do," I whisper to her, my chest starting to feel tight.

I want more than anything to be able to *do* something. To help her. To find a pill that will make her heart all better. But that's not how this works.

"Alright, Graham. It's time to go," Robb says.

I nod and look down at my mom's journal and open it up. The flyer for the Snail Kite contest falls out.

I know it sounds silly, but I feel like if I can find this bird it'll make everything alright. It all happens for a reason, right?

"Stay strong, Graham," the nurse says as he walks me to the door.

"Robb? I have one more favor to ask."

LET'S GO!

WHILE IT'S NORMALLY THE PITS, LOADING UP MY BACKPACK TODAY ISN'T something I'm dreading. It's not about jamming it full of things to distract me from waiting rooms. Instead, I've taken out any and all hospital stuff and I'm filling my bag with my binoculars, the marsh map, an extra Dom and Son T-shirt, and enough water for an entire soccer team. Before zipping it up, I remember to grab plenty of bug spray and sunscreen, as I've already learned my lesson on both. You never forget scratching a sunburnt bug bite.

"Where are you going?" Nick asks, when I make a beeline through the living room to the sliding door.

"Out," I say.

"Nu-uh. Zane and DJ's mom is almost here." Nick is sitting on one of the recliners with his pillow in his lap, and a sleeping bag on the floor next to him.

"Yeah . . . I'm not going over there with those guys."

"You have to, my dad said."

"Listen, I know it was you and your friends that tried to ruin my canoe. And I didn't tell your dad anything," I say. "So as far as I'm concerned, you owe me one. Just tell whoever asks that I went to Sarasota with your dad."

I hear the crunch of the gravel as a car pulls down the driveway, followed by a few quick beeps of the horn.

Nick seems like he's about to say something, but instead he turns and heads out through the front door. "Whatever."

I leave out the sliding back door, locking it with my spare set of keys. Part of me does feel bad keeping this from Dom, but I figure I'll be back ordering Swansen's before sundown.

He'll understand that I have to find a Snail Kite, that I have to do this for my mom. He'll understand. I know it.

Nurse's Station

Ding dong.

I take a deep breath in. There's no response, so I try again.

Ding dong.

I anxiously look into the doorbell video camera and mouth "Lou?" If this plan is going to work, I need her to be home.

Ding-ding-ding dong.

I push the doorbell one final time, Lou-style, in case it didn't work right at first.

I wait for what feels like a long time. A minute? Two?

Even though it feels a little creepy, I shield my eyes from the sun and take a peek inside the window at the top of the front door. It doesn't look like there are lights on or anything.

"Is this even the right house?" I whisper to myself, embarrassed.

I walk back down the front sidewalk toward the far edge of the driveway to look for clues, and, sure enough, Lou's bike is leaned up against the side of the garage.

So this is her house. Maybe she's not home?

I sigh and tighten the straps on my backpack. Maybe she *is* home, and maybe she doesn't want to come out.

I turn and start walking toward the street. I'm nearly at the end of the driveway when I hear the front door open. "Graham?"

I turn and there she is. It looks like she just woke up from a nap.

"Oh hey, Lou!" I say, jogging over.

"Hey," she says, protecting her eyes from the sun.

"You know friends at least text or call other friends back," I try to joke. But as soon as the words come out of my mouth, I regret them. Lou looks rotten. Things with her dad must be hard, but I don't quite know how to take it back. "Dom fixed our canoe," I offer up instead.

"I'm sorry, Graham. Really," Lou says. "Things at the hospital are complicated and—"

"Say no more," I say. "I get it. But we have something more important to talk about." I pull out my phone and show her the birding app.

"Do you see this? Six sightings in the last day. And less than twenty-four hours until the contest ends. We've got to find it before midnight. Today's the day."

"How did you figure out where I lived?"

I shrug, and she gives me the same look I once gave her, the one that means *for real, though.*

"Nurse's station," I say grinning. Once I explained the whole story to Robb, and I told him I knew what street—just not which house—he helped me look it up. "So, what do you say? Can we give it one more shot? For my mom and your dad? I can't shake the feeling that we're meant to find it."

Lou purses her lips.

"Wait here," Lou says. A few minutes later, she returns, wearing her birding outfit. She's even wearing her bucket hat from Loretta. The feather we found is stuck on one side. Her eyes are sparkling in the exact same way they did on the first day.

"I'll take the picture, and you can do the writing," I say. "I have a good feeling about today."

Lou smiles bright. "Let's go. We've got a Snail Kite to find."

THE BEGINNING

LOU AND I HEAD TO THE GARAGE TO GET OUR BOAT, WHICH HAS BEEN safely stashed to avoid further destruction.

"Got it?" I say.

"Got it."

We each grab a handle of the canoe and head out the back door of the garage, walking through the early afternoon heat. It feels like I'm doing a lot of the dragging, and by the time we make it to the dock Lou is breathing heavily. We finally drop the canoe next to the dock at the edge of the water.

"Graham, are you at all nervous about this?" Lou says. "We're heading deep in there. If something happens to one of us, something bad . . ." She doesn't finish her thought. "You're not afraid?"

Normally, I would be very afraid in a time like this. And usually I'd sit and wait for something or someone to tell me what my life is going to look like. But what if I could decide that myself?

"I am absolutely scared," I say. "Terrified, even!"

Lou smirks, cheered up for even a brief second.

Somewhere nearby we can hear a woodpecker tapping away, and the mixed symphony of other birds calling out to one another.

Lou lets out a big breath. "You're right. Let's go!"

We put on our life jackets and sit down on the dock, putting our feet on the floor of the canoe. We place both of our surprisingly heavy backpacks in the center of the canoe.

"You mind steering?" Lou says, crawling her way off the dock and onto the front seat. I do the same, teetering back and forth. I try to make small movements with my shoulders so we don't tip over before the trip even begins, and eventually ease down into my seat.

We're less wobbly than before, and it seems like we know what we're doing. We take a few paddles forward and our *J* strokes are strong and capitalized. Lou has the map open with her in the front of the canoe. Everything around us feels bright and full of life.

I just know we're going to find our bird.

LOU'S WORLD

"SOMETIMES THIS PLACE DOESN'T FEEL REAL," LOU SAYS. "LIKE IT'S A dream or something. Another planet we get to visit in a canoe."

"Totally."

I look around at the tall, skinny trees and the water lilies that dot the water in beautiful clusters on either side of us. There are large white birds swooping down in search of fish—herons, Lou says—and I can't help but feel like this place is pure magic.

"You know, I think I might owe you an apology," Lou says.

"About what?"

"For disappearing." Lou turns around and looks at me with a guilty expression, like she doesn't know what to say next. Luckily, I think I understand.

"Say no more," I say, waving my hand. "Sometimes I need a break from the world, too. Actually, sometimes I go to this place in my head when it all gets too much."

At this, Lou's eyes go wide. "Me too!"

"Wait, really? Does yours happen to be an ugly waiting room?" I ask with a nervous laugh.

I've never told anyone about My Waiting Room before. Honestly, I'm still slightly worried Lou might think it's too weird.

"No, no waiting room. Mine is sort of, well . . . a hiding place," Lou says. "It started when I was little. I'd go to this huge old oak tree in my backyard. It had this disease, so half of it was slowly dying, and everybody but me thought it was disgusting. I loved it. I'd go climb up the stinky, wide branches and lay on my back and close my eyes and go wherever I wanted. My parents chopped it down, but I still go there in my mind."

"What's it like? Where you go hide," I say. "I'm picturing ferns one thousand feet tall, gators that talk, and sky that looks like glitter."

"I think all those burgers are ruining your brain," Lou says, rolling her eyes. "It's hard to describe my hiding place. It's always kind of different," she continues. "Sometimes it was like I was really tiny and everything else was monstrously huge. Or I was on my own planet, and everyone else I knew was on their own, but we'd only keep getting further away from each other."

"Whoa," I say.

As we coast down our swampy inlet there are tons of different birds calling out to each other. I can't really tell the difference between one from the other, but I think of Gary from the swamp and how he just likes the pretty noises. He's right, it is nice. Like listening in on old friends catching up.

"A while ago I'd have dreams about the bad stuff, constantly. It felt like I couldn't even escape to my hiding place."

"You have strange dreams, too?" I ask.

"Oh, all the time. They used to be scarier, but I just told myself to cut it out."

"I didn't know that was an option," I reply with a laugh.

Neither of us are paddling, and we're slowly inching forward with the subtle current.

"You ever have good dreams?" Lou asks, still facing me.

"I think I used to, at least more than now."

"Just the other night I dreamt Loretta and I were feeding peanuts to hundreds of Scrub-Jays. Maybe even a thousand. More and more just kept coming," Lou says, closing her eyes for a second.

"There were so many they started to lift me off the ground. Like I was flying. All I could hear was the sound of their wings flapping, so many small noises that all turned into something bigger and louder. It was all I could hear. And it was amazing."

I look up, imagining Lou free and happy. When I look at her, I can see her eyes are still closed, tears streaming down her face. The breeze picks up, the trees rustling. I can almost hear a million wings flapping around us. Almost.

Bird Facts

"Hey, we're getting close," I say as I realize we're fast approaching the third bridge—the entrance into the Salvato Marsh. I dip my paddle in the water, and it makes a soft whooshing sound as our boat changes course to the right. I glance back to see the tiny trail of bubbles we're leaving behind.

"This is where Dom and I stopped before. It's the start of the maze that should lead us to the island."

The terrain ahead of us looks intimidating. The twisted, weathered trees hanging over us have to be over a hundred years old.

Lou wipes the tears from her cheeks and leans forward, opening up her backpack. She grabs the map from the visitor's center as I reach for my mom's journal in my own bag.

We compare both maps. I glance at some Sugarland moss just to make sure we're going in the right direction.

"Looks good," we agree.

We keep the map and journal laid out on the floor of the canoe next to our backpacks, so we can reference them easily.

"Here we go," I say, readjusting my grip on my paddle. "Uncharted territory."

Lou spins forward and we both dig our paddles into the water. After a few *J* strokes, we're cruising confidently.

On either side of us are lots of ferns, covering this section of swamp floor in lush green. Everything is different every few hundred feet. There are some tiny patches of prairie, where the sun is able to break through the thick tree cover. Then there are stretches that feel like we're in total darkness, vines and roots all around us. My eyes are constantly moving, scanning the water between paddle strokes, then the trees, then back to the water. I'm drenched in sweat. Even the trees look like they're sweating.

Nearly fifteen minutes pass before one of us speaks.

Ahead of us, on a branch above a patch of water speckled with sunlight, is a bird at the shoreline, taking quick steps with its webbed feet. Its bill is different from most birds, in that it looks like it curves upward.

"Wow, I think that's an Avocet," Lou says, studying her birding guide before pulling out her dad's camera to snap a photo. I reach for my binoculars and zoom in.

"Bird fact: *avocado* was taken, so they had to go with the backup name."

The bird continues swiping its beak back and forth in the shallow water, then gracefully flies off in search of another foraging spot.

"Not even the birds stick around for your quote-unquote facts." Lou smirks.

We keep paddling, and soon, on either side of us, we're next to big trees that are coming up from the water.

"These must be bald cypress," Lou says, looking up and shielding her eyes from the late-day sun. "Maybe pond cypress, too. My mom told me a hundred years ago they cut a ton down for, like, shingles for houses."

The trees above us are very tall and have huge bases, with mucky roots that stretch out underneath our canoe.

"We did a whole month of homeschool on how badly humans messed everything up down here. We probably could've done a whole year, to be honest."

Some of the trees looming over us look healthy at the top, providing shade with their canopy. But others look old and dead, their bare branches crooked and black.

"This is kind of eerie," I say.

"No kidding," Lou says. "Eerie . . . and awesome." She grins back at me.

I smile in agreement as we push forward together, our boat drifting over the surface of the canal. We follow the twisting waterway, and I glance down at the map with hopes that we can remember the path back out.

We come around a bend in the waterway and finally we have lots of room on either side of us. It's almost like a big pond. But the center of it is so deep you can't see the bottom. It looks dark and mysterious, like something you'd find on Venus or Jupiter.

"A sinkhole, nice," Lou says. "My parents taught me all about 'em last winter. When water mixes with the limestone that's underneath us. You give it enough time and it dissolves away till you're left with this."

On the far side is a huge fallen oak tree, at least six feet around at the uprooted trunk. It's fallen into the water at a nearly perfect forty-five-degree angle; its branches are sticking out of the water, serving as hazards for boats and napping spots for turtles. We maneuver toward the giant tree, trying to avoid shallow parts that'll get us caught up on branches.

"Want to hop out for a second to get a better look? We can pull the canoe up on these branches," Lou says.

We gently paddle up to the big fallen tree, and soon the bottom of our boat is rubbing on an algae-covered branch, leaving the nose of our boat just sticking out of the water. Lou grabs one of the branches above the water and hoists herself on top of the fallen tree. Her shoe nearly slips for a second, but she pulls herself up to the top. I put my canoe paddle down and take Lou's outstretched hand.

UNINVITED GUESTS

"ONE, TWO, THREE," SHE SAYS, HELPING PULL ME UP AS I TAKE A LONG stride out of the boat. The canoe wobbles in the water, but it doesn't go anywhere. We start climbing up the huge tree that's fallen into the water, like it's a natural broken drawbridge.

We're about fifteen feet from the ground, and from this height I can faintly make out seashells along the shallow banks of the water.

"Did I ever share that story that Gary told me? About the Fossil?" I ask Lou as we both finish climbing up the fallen tree. We turn around to look out at our little pond.

"I can't say that sounds familiar. What is it?"

"The Fossil."

"And again I ask, what is it?"

That's weird to hear Lou say that. I could swear it's something I've said myself.

"Hello? Earth to Graham?"

"Oh, yeah. The Fossil. It's a huge, super-old gator that escaped when they were filming a movie down here. It's apparently monstrous, like one of the biggest ever. It can eat an entire herd of cattle."

We look at the water, which is very still. Almost too still.

Crrrack!

Something small moves at the shoreline to our right, snapping a branch, and we both jump like it's a shark attack. We say nothing for a few seconds, and I can feel my heartbeat racing.

As we watch a baby squirrel run up a tree we burst into a fit of laughter.

"I wonder how many herds of cattle that little baby squirrel is eating today?" Lou jokes. "But seeing these shells makes me realize we need to find apple snails. Why didn't we think of that before? We find those, we find our Snail Kite. That's mainly what they eat."

"I think there's a little shell drawing on my dad's map," I say, trying to recall all of the hand-drawn pictures. "Let's double-check."

We carefully shuffle down the peeling bark of the fallen tree, holding onto stubby branches like stairway banisters. Lou heads toward the canoe first, shimmying down the peeling bark before hopping onto the boat.

"Like a swamp gazelle," I say, snapping a photo of her awkwardly tip-toeing out.

I go next, scooting down on my backside while trying to stretch out until my feet can touch the floor of the boat. I'm basically giving myself a wedgie, and I probably look like one of the knobby-kneed birds we've seen today.

"Majestic," Lou says through giggles, snapping a photo of me.

"Keep laughing," I say, finally making it back into the canoe with only a few scrapes. The boat is wobbling from side to side, so I sit down as fast as I can. Lou turns her phone screen toward me. I look like a very uncoordinated Flamingo that's also afraid of water.

"Think the contest will take this instead of the Snail Kite?" Lou giggles. "The judges will surely be able to tell by this creature's shockingly white thigh that this is a rare sighting. This species has migrated from Buffalo for the season."

"Two hundred and fifty words won't be enough for something so fantastic," I say. Our laughter echoes over the channel and off the cypress trees.

We quiet down and begin to notice a different, new noise.

"Do you hear that?" Lou asks me as she picks her paddle out of the water.

I cup my hand around my ear and listen to a low roar in the distance. It seems to be getting louder and closer.

"What is that?" asks Lou. "Is that the alligator?"

"I don't think so," I say.

I start getting a tingly feeling, like I'm going down a huge hill on a roller coaster. We paddle out to the center of the sinkhole, right above the seemingly bottomless pit.

We both have our eyes fixed on the direction of the noise when a boat finally comes into view. It's Nick, his friends, and their shiny boat barreling straight for us.

WRONG WAY

"WELL, LOOK WHO IT IS," SAYS DJ, WHO'S DRIVING THE BOAT. "I'VE NEVER seen a sorrier canoe, and that's the whole truth."

His taller brother, Zane, is next to him, and they're both wearing white hats turned backward, sunglasses, and black-and-red rashguard shirts. Only Nick is wearing a life jacket, a blue vest over his lime-green Dom and Son T-shirt.

"That's one ugly boat," Zane adds, nodding at the canoe's patched spot.

"An ugly boat that's unsinkable!" shouts Lou.

"I had a feeling we'd find you out here," DJ says, as their boat circles around our canoe. "You should just go home. You've got no chance at winning this cash."

"You don't seem to get it. We don't care about the money," Lou shouts back. She's gripping her canoe paddle tightly.

Their boat begins to gain speed as DJ continues to make circles around our canoe, leaving behind a choppy wake.

"Go try to intimidate somebody else, we're busy finding a Snail Kite," Lou says. "Nice to see you, too, Nick."

He's sitting on the bench in the back of the all-white boat but doesn't say anything back to Lou. He's staring at his feet, avoiding us.

"Y'all don't even know which way you're headed," says Zane, looking at his phone. "This says here the Shark Kite was sighted not even twenty minutes ago."

"You don't even know the name," I say.

"You're right. I don't care enough. So, it means nobody will miss it after we add it to the extinct species list," Zane says, plucking a fist-size rock from the floor of their boat.

"You couldn't hit a Waffle House with that thing," Lou says, standing up. She's still clutching her paddle, and the canoe is teetering back and forth.

"Oh yeah?" says Zane, who tosses the rock at our boat and us. It hits the plastic side of the canoe with a heavy thunk.

"Chill out, man, that could've hit us," I bark.

"Maybe the next one will," DJ threatens.

Bigger and bigger waves are forming all around us.

"Guys?" Nick says, finally muttering something.

"Don't worry, we got this," says Zane.

With a roar of the engine they take one final pass around us, creating near tsunami-level conditions. Waves are churning in every direction, and this once-quiet pond is now a wave pool.

"Whoa!" I shout as a monster wave rolls over the side of our canoe. Water fills our canoe and it teeters violently. Another wave follows, tipping our boat and throwing us completely underwater.

Our life jackets bring us back up quickly, but our canoe is totally capsized. Our backpacks are still floating and I grab them both with one arm, clinging to the overturned canoe with the other. Lou and I are both thrashing our legs in the water.

Nick's friends burst into laughter as they start to speed away.

"Good luck. You're gonna need it!" Zane hollers.

"Nick!" I shout, furious. "Come back!"

"Graham! Look!" calls Lou.

I follow her eyes, which are focused on the center of the pond. I watch as my mom's journal, with the Salvato Marsh map tucked inside, starts to sink.

"No!" I holler. I let go of the canoe and swim over to it as quickly as I can. I take a big breath and try to dive down to save it, but as my outstretched hand nearly touches the leather cover my life vest yanks me back up to the surface.

There's nothing else I can do but watch as my mom's journal starts to

      sink

               sink

                         s

                         i

                         n

                         k

And then, in an instant, it's gone. Its cover has disappeared, and I'm left looking at only fuzzy darkness below. My stomach twists. I can't believe it. My mom's journal is gone forever—along with the directions out of this place.

All Ashore

My eyes dart in every direction, searching for alligators or snakes in the water that we're now a part of. I tread water, spitting out a gulp I accidentally swallowed. I feel like I'm being sucked down with the journal. Like the undercurrent of dread is finally here to pull me under once and for all.

But I can't let that happen. Today is our day.

"Let's get to dry land," I say to Lou as I make it back to the capsized boat.

"Ya think?" she answers, her hair stringy and drenched.

The waves begin to calm down as Lou and I turn the canoe right side up. It halfway fills with water but manages to stay afloat. We put our backpacks, paddles, and Lou's hat inside the boat. We swim back to the tree where we'd just climbed, lugging our boat with us. I'm in the back, pushing the canoe forward with my shoulder and keeping an eye out for anything getting ready to eat us.

Lou gets to the old fallen oak tree first and scrambles up from the water. Instantly she reaches for her phone, pulling it from her drenched backpack.

"Oh no," she says. "No-no-no-no-no!"

I wedge the canoe under a branch and join Lou on the oak.

She's frantically pushing every button on her phone, but it's not doing anything. The screen is still black. I pull out my phone from my soaking wet bag and see it has suffered the same fate.

"It's a goner," Lou says. "Completely soaked. My dad's camera, too. Those guys are worse than pond scum."

"My phone's dead, too," I say, shaking it.

We listen to the caw of a Raven not far from us, as the water returns to a normal, tranquil state. We both open our backpacks and remove the soaked contents.

"What do we do now, Graham?" Lou says, hanging her spare sweatshirt from a jagged branch. "We don't have a map."

I'm not sure what it is, but it feels like something is brewing inside me. It's weird.

"Maybe we don't need one," I say. "You know something? I'm not scared, because we have bird facts."

"A bird fact coming from you actually does scare me."

"No, I'm serious. If I've learned anything it's that birds adapt. They figure it out, make it work," I say, wringing out my wet Dom and Son T-shirt. "Are we going to give up, or are we going to do the same?"

Mosquitoes start swarming around us, but thankfully our bug spray floats. I spray any and all visible skin and toss the bottle to Lou.

"Graham, I love the enthusiasm, really I do," she says, looking up at the sky in a mist of DEET. "But we're lost. We don't have phones or a map. And I don't know if you've noticed, but it's getting late. This is serious, we could die out here."

Lou is kind of right. While we do have more daylight, when you're surrounded by trees you lose your visibility much faster.

But we still have some time.

"My mom said their island was surrounded by cypress trees, so we must be close, right? If we turn back now, don't you think we'll always wonder if the Snail Kite was out there waiting for us? Besides, what do we have to get back to, more sitting around in hospitals?"

Lou sizes up all the trees around us, turning her head like an owl. She brings her pair of binoculars up to her pale eyes.

"Look, this is Sugarland moss. And it only grows on one side of these trees," I say, pointing to a patch of trees half-covered in fuzzy moss. "Nick and those guys went the other way, south. I think Dom was telling me we should head north."

"If we want to go that way, those trees do look like the oldest growth," she says, pointing toward a wavering outcropping of cypress. "Plus, there's a little opening. It looks like it could be a nice buffet spot for snails."

Lou starts stuffing her backpack full of her wet belongings.

"We have to be quick, okay?" she says. "My parents will flip once they realize they can't get a hold of me."

"We'll be so fast. If we don't see anything, we bolt," I say. I pause for a second before adding, "You're the best."

Lou offers up a small smile. I'm grateful she's not giving up yet on the Snail Kite—or on me. We head to our canoe and turn it to its side, letting the greenish water flood out. We flip it back over and keep it halfway in the water and halfway lodged against a few branches.

As Lou and I shimmy back into the boat, I can't help but feel like I finally get what it means to have a best friend. Not just a friend, a best one. It's something I haven't been able to describe before, but for the first time it's something that's mine. And that's better than a journal. After all, it's impossible to lose it in a swamp. Or even by an ice machine.

ON OUR OWN

"Maybe we should turn back. Each one of these little islands looks exactly the same," I say to Lou, my eyes scanning the horizon ahead.

Lou and I are staring forward as the waterway splits in two, surrounding what looks like a sizable island.

"Let's give it another minute," Lou says.

At that moment, there's a huge gust of wind, and in the center of the island I can see the tops of some trees blowing in the breeze. As the trees move, I see a few bright pops of white among the dark and drab wood.

"Let's get out here. We can be quick," I say, steering us toward the grassy shore. "I have a good feeling about this one."

We head toward shore and Lou hops out, splashing in the shallow water. I put my paddle in the middle of the canoe and bounce in after her. When you're completely covered in swamp water, the prospect of more swamp water isn't so bad.

We push our canoe out of the muck and onto a patch of burnt-out brown grass next to a large dirt mound. I can see the patched hole in the canoe and feel angry at Nick and his friends once again. I'm grateful, though, that Dom's patch job is holding up.

The trees around us are thick, but after a few steps I see something that might be the start of a little dirt pathway.

"Lou, over here. This might be something," I say, waving her over. It is definitely a worn trail of some kind.

"Animals?" Lou guesses, pulling up next to me.

"Something made this, alright."

We start walking in toward the oldest patch of cypress trees and quickly see that the path is overgrown. It doesn't seem like too many people use it. As we turn a long corner, we cut through densely packed cypress trees and see something in the center of the tiny island: a solitary tree, covered in beautiful blossoms.

"It's the magnolia tree!" I shout to Lou. "This is my parents' spot!"

I give a screech that sounds like a jubilant bird call.

"Oh my gosh! We made it!" Lou hollers, throwing her backpack high in the air in celebration. We jump up and down together, high fiving and hollering. It feels like fate.

We step through rows of cypress and get closer to the magnolia tree. I can now see the other tree by its side: the black olive. It looks awful. It's maybe twenty feet tall with half of it forming a pyramid shape with leaves. But the other half of it is singed and stripped of its bark. It definitely hasn't been alive for a while.

"What do you think happened?" Lou asks, running her hand over the black ash-covered bark on one half of the tree.

"Lightning?"

"Well at least the other one your parents planted is thriving," Lou says.

I can't seem to pull my eyes away from the singed trunk. "Yeah. I guess at least there's that," I say.

"Let's keep exploring," Lou says. "Come on."

We go around another bend in the trail and come to a small clearing. In the center is a rock firepit with a circle of big logs for seating around it. It's overgrown, but it's cool. Like I'm getting to see a time capsule from my parents' lives. I sit down on one of the huge tree rounds.

"Thanks, Dad. Thanks, Mom," I whisper, letting out a big breath. "And you too, Dom."

"Graham, I've got some bad news, unfortunately," Lou says, staring into her open backpack. "Our flashlights got ruined by the water, too."

"What does that mean?"

"That means we're about to: enter the swamp in the dark, in a canoe that may or may not sink, all without the use of a map."

I gulp and look around. The sun is well below the tree line and the light is fading fast. She's totally right, we'll get lost in a second.

"It also means that I'm happy at least one of us is a planner that brought waterproof matches," Lou says, revealing a tiny rectangle box in her hand like a backwoods magician. "Let's start making a fire. I think we might be here for the night."

Together Again

"I remember Dom saying that if we want to keep animals away, we could make a huge bonfire," I say, trying to focus my brain as it races with thoughts of alligators chasing us. "If anything's out there, that's our best chance at keeping it away from us."

"Are you sure?"

"Animals hate smoke. It's instinctual."

"Just like you instinctively hate wearing more than one pair of shorts for a summer," Lou says, starting to gather kindling for a fire. "Now start searching for some bigger, dried-out stuff that'll burn easily."

She drops her first armful of sticks in the center of the firepit, then heads over to the lightning-struck olive tree. One side of the bark is smooth, and the other one crisped by flames. Lou breaks off a blackened strip that looks like ash.

"This should do it," she says, heading to her bag to grab the pack of waterproof matches. I follow her to the firepit and pile together a handful of dry sticks.

After a few burnt matches, we're able to get a fire going. Lou and I take turns slowly adding sticks, then small branches, then small logs to the blaze. Soon it's up to our knees as the sky above turns to a dusky twilight.

I grab a handful of dry twigs and kneel next to the fire, watching the flickering yellow-and-orange flames. I toss them in and sit back on one of the logs. I imagine my dad and Dom rolling these out here years ago.

"This should be big enough to scare off anything trying to come this way," Lou says as she stokes the fire with a long branch. It gives a few pops, and burning embers twist up into the humid evening sky.

As the fire grows brighter, I can feel my clothes begin to finally dry out from before. Lou has laid her vest and hat out on a stump to dry them out.

"Come sit over here with me, Graham. We need to remember every second of this."

Dancing flames cast gentle shadows across my parents' island. It's a nice evening, and the sky is a glowing Creamsicle kind of orange. It smells like decomposing trees and bog water and different flowers blooming all around us.

"If I made my own planet, I'd want every evening to look like this," I say to Lou.

She doesn't say anything right away and lies back on one of the large logs, her hands clasped behind her head. Frogs and toads are croaking all around us. The air is still heavy and hot, but a small breeze blows over our island.

"You know, at this moment right now, I couldn't care less that we didn't find anything for that contest," she says.

"Me too, actually," I answer, leaning back with her. My armpits smell *awful*. "So what if we don't see that bird and win? This place is like magic."

I scoop up a handful of dirt and stuff it into my pocket. If this place is magic, maybe bringing a little soil back for my mom and her heart might not be a bad idea.

Grrrrrrt. Grrrrrrrrrrrrt.

We hear a low rumbling in the darkness. It's something different than the animals that have been calling to us all day. It sounds deep and scary, like the growling of a wounded animal. Lou and I look at each other, our eyes both filled with panic.

Bub. Bub. Burtttttttb.

Then, it stops.

We hear a branch snap, then the flapping of wings in the dark. We listen to a series of small splashes, then the water goes silent again.

"Is it the Fossil?" Lou whispers to me, her voice quiet and shaky.

We look down the path, and soon we hear the sound of more branches rustling and breaking. I swear I can see glowing eyes in the distance.

"What is that?" I whisper to Lou. It's dark and scary out here at nightfall, and whatever is coming our way doesn't seem to be afraid of our fire.

"Hello?" Lou calls toward the path. We huddle together and can hear the noises get closer and closer.

Something is coming up the path. It's headed right for us.

"Go! Get away!" I shout out, but a large shadowy figure soon comes into view of the firelight.

Then, a burst of light.

"Guys?" says whoever is carrying the bright flashlight.

It turns upward, revealing a face: it's Nick.

OWE YOU ONE

"What do you want?" Lou says, shielding her eyes from the bright light. "Your friends send you out here to finish their dirty work for 'em?"

"They're not my friends anymore," Nick says, taking a few steps toward us and the fire. He's wearing an orange life jacket from his stash in the garage. "And I'm sorry for earlier. It felt like everything was happening so fast . . . it was like I couldn't do anything to stop it."

"Yeah, right," Lou replies. "You could've done plenty."

"When I saw the way they were treating you, I felt responsible for it. I felt, um, guilty," Nick stammers. "Then when they flipped your boat and left? Nobody deserves to be treated like that. Besides, it's dangerous."

Lou narrows her eyes, unconvinced.

"So now you feel bad? Right after you help those guys get a photo so you can get your cut of the prize money?" she shoots back. "Funny how that works."

"Believe what you want. I realized today I should never have bailed on you from the beginning. But I'm here now," Nick stammers. "I knew you guys were going to be stranded, so I came out looking for you."

Nick's flashlight is focused on the ground in front of him, and I can see his face in the flames of our campfire. We lock eyes. He seems gloomy and sad, like how he looked when we drove past his mom's do-over family.

"My boat has lights on it, and we can make it back before it's pitch black out," Nick explains. "Then you're both free to hate me forever. I'm sure I'll be grounded for years for this, so it's not like you'll be seeing much of me anyways."

I look at the popping fire that's slowly starting to dwindle, already burning through our tiny supply of dried wood.

"You're right, you're here now. We can deal with everything else once we make it home," I say. "Let's get out of here."

I'm a little sad to leave, even though I know it's for the best. Since I've been in Sugarland I've learned that the summertime creatures sleep during the hot days, then go absolutely wild during the nights. We *need* to go.

"I guess leaving seems like the smart thing to do," Lou finally concedes. "My parents are probably worrying about me."

"My phone is in the boat and sometimes you can randomly find service out here. We can text your parents so they know where you are," Nick reassures.

From another nearby island comes a terrifying sound.

Squeeeealll!

"What was that?!" Lou asks.

"I think it was like a wild hog or something," I say, swiveling my head in nearly every direction. "Whatever it was, it sounded scared. Like it was running away."

We pause, listening.

Hissss.

That sound is different. And definitely not a wild hog.

"Okay, yeah. It's time to go," Lou says.

I feel a nervous sweat forming on my forehead.

We start taking the path back to our canoe and Nick's boat, passing by the trees that my parents planted. This time I spot something different, though.

"Huh, look at that," I say, going over to the black olive tree. Off one of the petrified branches is new growth, a resilient little tree sprouting from the harshest of conditions.

Nick and Lou forge ahead, and I speed up to rejoin them—just as they both stop dead in their tracks.

"Graaaaham," Lou says in a very slow, drawn-out way. Nick is frozen, his flashlight pointing straight ahead.

"What?" I say, nearly stumbling into them both. I peer over Lou's shoulder only to see the biggest alligator I've ever seen, its eyes glowing a terrifying red.

Hissssss.

Its jaws are open wide, exposing huge, pointy teeth. It hisses at us again, or at least in our direction. It's honestly longer than the Blue Beast and nearly just as wide.

Which can only mean one thing.

This is . . .

Hissssssssssssssss.

"The Fossil. It has to be. And that means that huge dirt mound by our canoe is its, its—" Lou stammers, slowly backing up. "Nest."

The alligator is halfway in the water, and we can barely see the end of its tail. It's staying still for now. One thing's for certain: we're trapped.

"I can't believe we didn't see that before," Lou adds.

Overhead, we hear a bird squawking. The Fossil turns its scaly head in the bird's direction. The alligator's head is covered with battle scars. I really hope it doesn't eat Snail Kites . . . or contestants looking for them that are under the age of thirteen.

"Let's back away slowly and quietly," I whisper. Each noise we make seems magnified, and after I crack a twig in half the gator makes another terrifying sound, a deep and guttural roar. My entire body is shaking like a leaf.

We slowly creep away, careful to be quiet, and return to the bonfire area in the center of the island. I can feel blood pumping at the sides of my head.

"The Fossil wants to guard its nest," Nick says. "If we make a big enough fire it shouldn't come up to us. It's too busy playing defense."

"Lot of defense talk for a guy who always skips football practice," I say drily.

"Har," Nick replies. "And we'll be without a phone all night. We're not going near that boat."

Lou isn't cracking. She is serious. "You're right. They're nocturnal. If we can make it through the night without being gator food, it'll leave for a morning swim," Lou says. "Then we can take our boat back, and Captain Backstab over here can return by himself."

The swamp around us is starting to make nighttime noises, each one a guessing game in potential fear. We can hear the splashing of water in the distance and the rustle of bats overhead.

"Come on, let's get firewood. We're all in this together," I say.

SECRET COMPARTMENT

THE SKY IS BRIGHT TONIGHT, LUCKILY. THE MOON IS NEARLY FULL AND hanging in the sky like a hazy orb. From a tree nearby, I hear the "hoo" of an owl. The air is warm and thick.

I think back to young Dom and my dad making this firepit all those years ago. How they'd be happy to see it getting put to good use. That we're not giving up on it.

"Wish I thought to bring some food," Nick says, staring into the bright coals of the fire. "Or a fishing pole at the very least. I'm super hungry."

My stomach growls at the mention of food. I'm hungry, too.

"Wait, I just remembered!" I blurt out, jumping to my feet. I take a few brisk steps toward my backpack and start unzipping all the tiny little pockets hidden throughout.

"Huh?" says Lou.

"We're saved! By candy!" I say. "I hide it in secret compartments for future hospital emergencies. Or when my mom eats my entire stash."

I reach an arm into a tiny zipper pocket and pull out a fistful of glorious treats.

"Jackpot!"

I grab several fun-sized pieces of chocolatey, miraculously still dry candy bars and toss them at Nick and Lou like a marshland Willy Wonka.

"Graham, you're a hero. A legend," Nick says, opening a piece after picking it up from the grass at his feet. We savor each bite, energized by caramel and nougat entering our bloodstream.

"Wait! Graham, check my bag. I think I threw some granola bars in there earlier this week," Lou says from across the fire, finishing off one of the chocolate/almond/coconut candies that only my mom likes.

I walk over to her opened bag and glance inside.

"I don't see anything," I say, a little uneasy digging through someone else's stuff.

"You're not looking hard enough then. Look in the inside sleeve-y thing."

I begin a full-on search-and-rescue for granola bars.

I unzip the pocket for the bigger compartment of her bag and see a few granola bars tucked into the sleeve where you'd normally have a laptop. I grab them, but behind them is a packet of folded paper. It's thick and held together by a few staples. I pull it out of Lou's bag and open the folded papers. The first cover page only has the logo for the Florida Clinic.

I turn it over, and I have to read, then reread, then re-reread what I'm seeing. At the top of the page it says: "Heart Transplantation for Children." It's the same sort of packet all new patients get. My mom got one when we went to the hospital that first day.

Which means . . .

THE TRUTH

"You lied to me!"

"About the granola bars? I mean, sure there's only two, but—"

"No! About this!" I say, holding the packet of heart-transplant information in my hand. Everything in my head feels like it's short-circuiting. I can barely see straight.

"You are here for your dad, right? That's why you're always at the hospital?"

Lou starts to look squeamish.

"Right?"

Lou tosses another stick onto the roaring fire and walks over toward me. She sits down next to me.

"Have a seat, Graham," she says.

"Not until you tell me what's going on," I say, my voice starting to shake.

Lou doesn't say anything until I sit next to her. She looks away from me, into the fire, then turns back. Tears are welling up in her eyes, and a few fall down her cheek.

"I'm not at the Florida Clinic for my dad. *I'm* the reason. He's there for me."

TRIPOD

My brain struggles to keep up as emotions swirl in my belly. All the anger and frustration that Lou lied to me are quickly evaporating and turning into something far more potent: fear.

"I don't know why I didn't tell you," Lou says, absentmindedly poking at the fire. "It started off unintentionally. I kept convincing myself I'd tell you the next time I saw you. But it was nice getting to be normal for a little bit."

She looks meek and so, so apologetic, but I can't get past the fact that she lied.

I shake my head, panic rising. "Do you know what sort of danger you're in? Forget gators and bird chases and everything. You're sick, and we're *trapped* out here."

Lou has no idea what she's done. She's put her health, her life, at risk and all because she agreed to go out and get stuck in a swamp with me.

"I didn't want to hide it from you. I swear. I figured I was going to tell you at some point."

"Yeah? And when would that be?" I spit out. "When you're prepping for your transplant surgery?"

"I don't know! I've actually been having fun for the first time in forever, so I truly don't know," Lou says. She nervously kicks a rock at her feet. "You saw me as a normal kid, and I liked it. I . . . guess I didn't want it to end."

I start thinking about every encounter Lou and I have had, how it's all suddenly thrown into a new light. I remember how tired her dad was at Swansen's. It was the face of someone exhausted. Not from being sick, but from loving someone through an illness.

"Your parents are probably losing it right now. You have no idea what it's like to love somebody and know that they could die at any possible moment. Now we're trapped by a giant gator all because of some pointless bird chase."

"Don't you dare say this was pointless, okay?" Lou shoots back. "I don't want to hear you say that. It's been the best adventure of my entire life. The only time that I haven't been the sick kid who can't leave the hospital without somebody constantly worrying."

I'm trying to get it, really I am. I just can't believe Lou would endanger her life for this and not tell me.

"I don't understand why you couldn't tell me," I say. "I can handle tough stuff, too. I've been dealing with these things forever."

Lou scoffs. "So, you know what it's like to give up your childhood? To be told at the start that everything works differently for you?"

"I mean, uh . . . yeah, actually!" I say, defensively.

"Urgh!" Lou says. "Face it, Graham, it's different. If it wasn't for me, you'd still be walking hospital hallways looking for ice. Admit it."

I'm quiet. Lou's words kind of hurt my feelings. Maybe because they're true.

Lou takes a few deep breaths. "When you're a sick kid there is no normal or okay. Everyone wants you to be their hero, or to put on a tough face, all while they forget I'm still only a kid. I'm tired of it. Sick and tired."

A silence hangs over the campfire.

"I know what you mean." Nick's voice breaks from the shadows. He's been silent for a while, so it's surprising to hear him.

"Oh yeah?" Lou says.

"The feeling that everybody wants something different and better. When everybody treats you like damaged goods," Nick continues. "Who wouldn't want to live a life like everybody else? You can't be mad at Lou for that, Graham."

"Wow," Lou says, sounding legitimately caught off guard. "Thanks."

She picks up a pile of dry brush and tosses it on the fire all at once. The flames dance dangerously high. With the bright flames I see Lou's face clearly. I can see how sad she is. Tears are streaming down her face.

"You know I see people, people like you, Graham Dodds. People who don't know what to do with the life they're supposed to live. And it makes me furious."

"What does that mean?" I ask.

"It means that when you're like me, when the worst is happening,

235

everything is clear," Lou says, her voice quivering. "You can either spend your time living in fear or searching for hope. Either way, life goes on whether you like it or not."

She's right. About the choices being clear. I mean, up until recently I spent all my time in a waiting room I've made up in my own brain.

Is that living?

Is that what Lou means?

The fire shifts, sending the smoke in our direction. I stand up, shielding my face from the fumes.

I take a breath.

"I'm sorry, Lou. Really."

"When you're sick, lots of people expect you to be like a character in a movie. Like I'm supposed to be a hero," Lou says. "I might be sick, but I'm a person. And I need to live my life while I've got one. You should, too."

I clench my teeth.

"Why? What's the point? It seems like all my favorite people are sick."

"So? Don't be so negative," Lou says, staring at the fire. "It could always end at any moment. That's what it means to actually be alive."

I look up and see that the stars are starting to come out. They're huge and bright. This far into the swamp, everything's brighter.

"It's funny, this morning I was supposed to go into the hospital and start on an IV drip until my transplant comes. They say it could happen any day. But they always just say that," Lou says. "And then it'll be goodbye life, goodbye normal stuff, goodbye fun. I'll be captured by a tube that's stuck in my arm, trapped in a room for the rest of my probably short life."

"But that means you're going to get a heart transplant soon, though, right? If you're at the top?"

"Yeah. Finally at the top of the list," Lou says with a sigh. "Worst of the worst."

"What's wrong with your heart?" I ask.

"It's a congenital disease. They found a hole in my heart when I was a baby," Lou says. "For kids like me, we get the special privilege of being diagnosed early and poked and prodded for an entire lifetime. Then they decide when the poking and prodding is done and when your heart needs to be replaced."

A wet log lets out a slow hiss from the fire.

"Before I even drank from a baby bottle, I had open-heart surgery. Not too many people can say that."

The three of us stare into the fire for a long moment. And I make a decision, since we're telling the truth. "I'm afraid of becoming an orphan," I say. "It's in my nightmares constantly. If I lost my mom, I don't know what I'd do."

The owl hoots again.

"Something tells me you'd figure it out," Lou says, sitting down next to me and nudging me with her shoulder. "You're never truly alone, Graham. Don't forget that. It's probably why your mom brought you back here. In case anything happened with her, you'd at least have a family."

Nick and I lock eyes, and in that moment, I feel like we understand each other. That no matter what might happen, when stuff goes bad we could still be there for each other . . . if we want.

"I'm glad I got to tell you guys," Lou says, settling into a notch in the log behind us.

"Yeah, me too."

I think about what Lou was saying, about waiting and everything. Maybe she's right. Maybe it's time to be done waiting.

The night calls of the marsh echo over the water. I listen to the world for a long time. Normally the wild night sounds would be frightening—but tonight it's like a lullaby.

"Think we'll see any more of the Fossil?" I ask Lou. But she doesn't answer, already asleep. She's using her still-damp backpack as a pillow, her back to the toasty fire.

I look over at Nick, who's fast asleep as well.

"Sweet dreams, everybody," I say, tossing on a few more huge logs to keep our fire raging through the night. I do my best to get cozy, using my life jacket as a pillow and my Dom and Son T-shirt as a blanket.

THE "YOU BELONG HERE" CLUB

I USED TO THINK LOU AND I WERE PART OF THE WORST CLUB IN THE WORLD. A club where membership is based on something horrible happening. A group for people who didn't want to be there. But right now? I don't know, maybe I'm seeing it differently for a change. Maybe it doesn't have to be so negative. Because everyone is going through their own hard stuff.

So tonight, by this fire and under these stars, maybe I'll start the "You Belong Here Club." It's a great club. Everybody's already a member, if they want to be. We can all go through the tough stuff together.

THE CALL

I OPEN MY EYES TO THE SOFT LIGHT OF A NEW DAY. I'M SURPRISED I SLEPT straight through the night. Birds are beginning to chirp, their eager morning calls filling the sky. The stars are gone, but the moon is still faint on the horizon. The fire is now a pile of faintly glowing embers with Lou curled up next to it, her whole body wrapped up in her sweatshirt.

"Lou?" I whisper. She doesn't move, so I do my best not to wake her. I glance at Nick, who's also still snoozing.

I sit up and take a look around, surveying our island. Through rows of thin pines, I can see the magnolia blossoms' vibrant white petals and the ashy remains of the olive tree.

The sun slowly rises over the swampy water. The clouds begin to glow in the morning light. It's like when you're in the hospital overnight, and you get to watch everything turn into a new day.

"Okay, here we go," I say. I stand up and give a yawning stretch, then start taking careful steps toward the edge of the water and our canoe.

I get to the base of a good climbing tree and start to scale the bottom branches. I pull myself up on the sturdy tree until I see our canoe and Nick's boat. They're both right next to the Fossil's nest. I wait and watch, doing my best to be silent. There's no sign of the alligator as the sun begins to rise higher in the clear sky. I carefully step down from the tree and make my way to the water. It seems the Fossil has left.

Then, I hear a call. Something familiar, but I'm not sure from where. A dream? I turn toward a fallen pine tree near Nick's boat. That's when I see it. A flash of a powerful orange beak biting into a fat, round snail.

I can't believe it. But it's real. I know it is.

The Snail Kite.

I freeze, studying every detail of the rare bird in front of me. It's bigger than I expected, with gray feathers and a white patch on its tail. I don't think I'll ever forget the bright-orange of its talons or the vibrant red of its eyes.

This bird is striking. Truthfully, it has to be the most beautiful and majestic thing I've ever seen. And that's an actual bird fact.

Screech.

My thoughts drift off to my mom and dad, all the memories they made here. It's always felt like I never got to share in any of them. Until now.

As I step forward, a branch cracks under my foot, and the Snail Kite looks in my direction. We lock eyes, and I can't help but shake the feeling that this bird came for me. To tell me something. I stand motionless and we stare at each other for a long time. The bird barely moves, curiously looking at me, imparting its secrets all while digesting snail guts. It takes a few hops forward and starts to give itself a bath in a small puddle of water.

Click!

From behind me I can hear the sound of a phone snapping a photo.

I look to see Nick crouched down on one knee.

Screech. Screech.

The Snail Kite flaps its wings and takes flight, cruising low over the water. I give a tiny wave, thankful for that magical moment.

"Sorry. Thought it was on silent when I got it from the boat," Nick says, slowly making his way toward me.

"No worries, man. It all happens for a reason."

"No sign of the Fossil?"

"None yet," I say.

"That's good. Listen, Graham, before we get out of here and go back home, I wanted to . . ." Nick says, fumbling for the right words. "For the first time maybe ever my dad and I actually talked about stuff with my mom. And tons more, too."

The sun begins to grow brighter, poking out over the tops of trees in the distance.

"I'm realizing I probably have you to thank for it," he says, his face covered in dirt. "My dad's not really good at talking about feelings, so it was quite possibly the strangest conversation I've ever had."

I give a little laugh, fully imagining what that talk was like.

"But he tried," Nick says. "So, thanks. Really. It means a lot."

I give Nick a nod. I can't help but feel some weird sense of relief.

Ding.

Nick's phone rings with a message, finally able to get service on this little corner of the island.

Di-di-di-di-di-ding!

More and more messages begin to come in, probably all texts from earlier.

"Graham," Nick says, staring at his phone.

"What is it?"

"I don't know how to say this."

"Just say it."

My pulse begins to race.

"It's your mom, Graham. My dad's been trying to contact me since midnight. Today's the day. She got the call. They found her a heart."

THE MESSAGE

IF MY MOM IS RIGHT, AND BIRDS ARE HERE TO DELIVER MESSAGES, I WONDER what my Snail Kite was here to tell me.

That nobody knows what the future holds.

That if you search for the magic, it will find you.

That everything is going to be okay.

Or maybe it's saying, "I have no idea what the message is, figure it out yourself."

I do know one thing; my waiting is over. At last.

I've been looking for the Snail Kite. But now I wonder if the Snail Kite has been looking for me.

LET'S GO!

"GRAHAM, CAN YOU HEAR ME?" SAYS NICK. HE'S WAVING AT ME, BUT IT sounds like I'm at the bottom of a swimming pool. His words are jumbled sounds, total gibberish.

Did he really say my mom's transplant is ready?

"Your mom's getting a new heart, man!" Nick says, snapping me back into reality. He howls into the morning sky. He's excited, and I've never seen him smile, really. He looks truly happy. It suits him.

A weird, half-stunned grin stretches over my face and stays there.

We hear Lou up from the firepit and watch as she makes her way down the path, her hair wild and messy.

"What's happening?" Lou says, joining us.

"Graham's mom got the call. They have a new heart for her," Nick says to Lou.

I watch as her eyes grow bright, and her face is lit up with a massive smile.

"Seriously?" she asks in disbelief.

I nod my head yes, but feel like I'm still asleep, still dreaming.

It's happening. It's really happening.

"We'll come back for your canoe later. We've got to get to the hospital. Now," Nick says, heading over to his boat. He pulls on the ripcord to start the motor.

Burburburburb.

Lou and I run back to the firepit and grab all our stuff. We pour the last of the drinking water on the smoldering coals.

"We'll be back," I say, looking around the island. "Promise."

I pass the magnolia, the black olive, and countless other trees as I follow Lou back to the water. I try to touch a few leaves on each tree. I don't know why, it just feels like something Gary and Loretta might tell me to do. We get back to Nick's boat, and Lou gives me her hand as we climb on board and throw on our life jackets.

"Ready?" Nick asks. "Here we go."

PILLOW FORT

WHEN I WAS LITTLE, I WOULD MAKE PILLOW FORTS ALL THE TIME. LIKE when you take all the cushions from the couch, the chairs from the dining room, and the breakable things from everywhere else and start to make a fort out of it all?

I loved doing that.

I used to spend days, if not weeks, inside all my creations. I'd dream up new lives and fantastic worlds, turning things like plain old couch cushions into ivy-covered castle walls.

But do you remember when, eventually, the dog would run through it all? It wouldn't know what it was doing, but it was ripping apart a world that existed only seconds prior.

I never thought that My Waiting Room would really end this way, but somehow it has. The walls toppling over. The two doors I've stared at forever tilting over like they're made of cardboard. All showing me something I should've known all the time—it's the same thing on the other side, no matter what door you're using to get there. It's all just a pillow fort in the middle of the room, something temporary.

And you know what? I like it all falling down. I'm ready to leave. Ready for whatever it looks like on the other side.

See You Later

After making record time coming back from Sarasota, Dom speeds the Blue Beast up to the emergency room entrance to the Florida Clinic and slams on the brakes. There are no fancy water fountains splashing at this doorway.

"See ya in there," he says, as we hop out of the van and sprint into the hospital, following arrows toward the cardiac wing. I'm breathing heavily, and all of our shoes are trailing mud across the freshly waxed floors of the hospital hallways.

"LaDonna!" I shout, seeing my mom's transplant coordinator we met on the first day. She's at a huge desk in front of two white, windowless doors.

"There you are, Graham! We've been looking for you all morning," she says, shuffling stacks of papers on her desk. "Your mom's about to be prepped for surgery. It's happening."

Her face changes when she sees Lou, though.

"Lou," she says, softly. "Did . . . did someone contact you?"

Lou looks puzzled. Nick's phone died as soon as we left our island, and Dom's battery went shortly after. "Our phones are all dead. I haven't heard from anyone."

"Didn't you hear?" LaDonna says quietly.

"Hear what?"

"Because of blood and body type we had to pass over some patients. Which means you're next," LaDonna says in a hushed voice. "Your heart is ready, too. Your parents have been notified and have been searching for you everywhere. Hold on."

As LaDonna makes a call on her phone, I turn to Lou.

She looks like nothing's happened, weirdly. Like normal.

"Thanks, Graham Dodds."

"For what?"

"For a normal day."

"Being trapped in a terror swamp by a giant gator feels normal?"

She smiles. It's small and scared, though.

"More than you'll ever know."

She hands me an orange-and-red friendship bracelet.

Fwooosh.

From doors leading to another waiting comes Lou's mom, frantically running to her daughter's side.

"Lou!" her mom screams, racing to hug her.

"Mom, I'm sorry we didn't—"

"It's alright, dear," Lou's mom says, cutting her off, holding Lou's cheek with her hand. "I think I get it."

"The bird. We found it," Lou says, a rush of tears welling in her eyes.

"I bet you did," her mom answers gently. "Your dad is on his way now. He was out looking for you. I swear he downloaded every birding app imaginable to try and find you."

"And you'll have to let him know his camera is toast," she adds with a sniffling laugh. She and her mom share another big hug as LaDonna swings around from her desk with a wheelchair for Lou to use.

"You had to be so worried. I'm sorry we were stuck out there. It's a long story," I say to Lou's family. "I had . . . no idea . . . about the transplant."

I'm searching for the right thing to say, but I can't seem to find it.

"Today might just be the good news we've all been waiting for, Graham," her mom says, giving me a pat on the shoulder.

LaDonna begins going over paperwork and procedures with Lou's parents, and my friend wheels herself toward me. She looks so small in the bulky wheelchair.

"Tell your mom I'll be thinking of her. Remind her it all happens for a reason," Lou says, the dirt from the swamp still streaked across her face.

"You'll have to let her know yourself, when you're both recovering."

"I'll see you later, Graham Dodds," Lou says. She reaches out and grabs my wrist with both hands. They feel cold and frail. I look into her eyes as she gives my arm a squeeze. Her parents walk over to her and grab the handles on the chair.

"Ready?"

"Ready," Lou says.

As they head toward the special doors, she turns back to me. "And Graham, one more thing. I've hidden seventy-nine origami frogs throughout this hospital. Have fun."

I smile as the doors close behind them.

"See you later, Lou."

A CHANCE

Nick and I race to the floor where my mom is being prepped. We go to the surgical waiting area and talk to someone behind the desk.

"I need to see my mom, she's about to get a new heart!" I say.

"What's the name?"

"Lindsay Dodds."

"It looks like we're almost ready. I don't know if I can let you go see her," says the woman behind the desk.

"Please. Just to say hi," Nick says. "It'd mean a lot."

"You have no idea what we had to do to get here," I say.

The woman looks up and stares at me for a long, hard moment. And maybe it's a bit of desperation in my eyes, or the fact that I'm covered in swamp muck and smell like a compost pile, but she grabs her key fob and gets up from her desk.

"Come with me and stick close by."

We get to my mom's room and there are people moving all around.

"Graham!" she says, her hair matted from lying in bed. "Oh, you made it."

Mom holds my hands.

"Sorry, everybody, it's time," says a person in a white coat.

"We found it mom, the island and the Snail Kite," I say. I don't tell her about Lou, not yet. "I brought back your island for you. It's in my pocket."

"It all happens for a reason," she says with a smile. "I love you. Now let's go get a new heart."

WAITING

YOU KNOW HOW, SOME DAYS, TIME DOES FUNNY STUFF? FOR EXAMPLE, amazing days seem to always go by too fast. Time blurs together, and then all of a sudden a whole day has passed. I think the last time I felt that way was meeting Gary and Loretta with Lou. How I never wanted that day to end.

Now it's the total opposite. Every passing moment is uncertain. Minutes and hours are blurring together, both taking a lifetime. It feels like that book Lou read on Norway, where their summers are total daylight and winters are nothing but darkness. You can never really tell what time it is. That's where I am right now, I think. A place where time is too fast and too short, where I continue to wait.

And wait.

And wait.

News

It's been nearly eight hours now, and time is starting to feel like it's moving backward. A few other families have arrived, and it's as if we're all in our own little world.

I've picked up some scrap paper and a pen from a table. I've started and stopped the sketch of the Snail Kite almost six times now. I never can seem to get it quite right.

Dom's been letting me use his phone, since mine got soaked. I've been looking at it every five minutes since my mom went into surgery hours ago. It says I've walked four miles today, and all of that's been from pacing back and forth down this hospital hallway.

Nick and Dom have been sleeping in chairs in the corner near me, and Lou's parents have been doing more pacing than me.

"Graham, want anything from the vending machines?" Dom asks, standing up to go find a snack. He didn't eat on the way back from Sarasota, so he's gotten a snack from the vending machine about four times now.

"No thanks, I'm good for now," I answer.

Dom starts walking away, then turns back.

"I want you to know you've always got a home with us, no matter what happens," Dom says, stumbling over the words a bit. "I mean it, kid. You're family."

Fwwwooosh.

Suddenly the windowless doors leading into the operating rooms open and a nurse in green scrubs comes out. It's Robb with two *b*'s. He has no idea how long I've waited for someone to walk through that waiting room door.

It's time. Time to find out our fate.

STILL IN THE WOODS

ROBB WALKS OVER TOWARD ME, AND NICK AND DOM STAND UP FROM THEIR chairs.

"You're all family?" the nurse asks.

Dom and I lock eyes and we both nod. Robb motions for the three of us to follow him through the doors.

It's kind of funny, you know, that I've been waiting forever for somebody to come out and tell me what's going on with my life. But in the end, I'm the one who has to walk through the door.

We step into the first room on our right, a tiny space with only a few off-white cabinets and chairs. LaDonna and a man in a white coat are already inside.

"Have a seat, everyone," LaDonna says. "This is the surgeon, Dr. Chen."

I sit down on the white plastic seat, and my whole body feels weak, like a strand of seaweed. I can barely catch my breath.

"Well, a lot still has to go right, but I think we can safely say we've got some good news for you," the surgeon says, peering over his thin glasses.

"Yeah?" I say, lightheaded.

"She is recovering after the surgery, which ultimately went well. If everything goes according to plan, you can see her in a few hours," Dr. Chen continues.

"You mean the surgery was a success!?" Dom says, a huge grin forming on his face.

"Yes, a success."

"*Awwwooo!*" Dom howls. He gives me a huge bear hug, then one for Nick.

I don't say anything. I'm in total shock.

"Now we're definitely not out of the woods yet. We had to put a balloon pump in to help along one chamber of the heart," Dr. Chen says. "We have to see how she responds."

"Right," Dom says, clearing his throat. I can tell he's trying to tone down his excitement.

"Plus organ rejection is very common," adds LaDonna. But I can tell she's happy.

A phone in Dr. Chen's pocket begins to make noises. He glances at the screen and his face looks serious.

"I'm afraid I have to go. But LaDonna will take it from here. More soon," the surgeon says with a nod before walking into the hallway.

"I know it can be scary right now, but this is great news. I'm so happy for you all, Graham," LaDonna says. "Still, you might not get to see her until tomorrow."

"I'll be right here until then," I say. I feel my shoulders relax.

I can't believe it. It happened. It really happened.

For the first time, maybe ever, I let myself feel a little sliver of something that feels suspiciously like hope.

DayDream

It's been an hour since the good news, and I'm full of tons of energy. Is this real? Is this the end of our journey that's taken us from Chicago to Seattle to Buffalo to here? Our new beginning?

I haven't been able to sit still, so I'm heading back from a trip to get snacks with Nick.

"Man, I'm so glad about your mom," Nick says to me, taking a sip of iced tea.

"How's yours, Nick?" I ask him.

"I don't really know."

"Maybe today's a good day to find out," I say. If I've learned anything in the swamp with Lou and over the last twenty-four hours, it's that you have to make the most of every moment you're given.

"Maybe you're right," he replies.

As we get back to the waiting area it's thinned out, with only me, Dom, Nick, and Lou's parents left. Luckily her dad made it to the hospital in time to see Lou before surgery.

Fwwwooosh.

The sound of the windowless doors open; all our eyes dart to them. Robb with two *b*'s enters the waiting area again, his expression unreadable. A nurse and a different doctor are in the hallway behind him.

Robb turns to Lou's parents and walks them toward the same room where we received our news. The doors shut behind them, and my eyes stay glued there expectantly.

Minute by minute passes and the doors remain shut. I wish I had X-ray vision so I could see what was happening back there. My mind is racing with each passing second. I can't wait for Lou's family to burst out to tell us the exciting news.

Fwwwooosh.

The doors open, and Robb is leading Lou's parents back to the waiting room. But something is different. Something is wrong. The room suddenly goes wobbly as I see Lou's mom collapse into her husband's shoulder. They both start crying and everything feels like it's in slow motion.

Oh no.

It's bad news.

NIGHTMARE

WE SIT IN STUNNED SILENCE. EVENTUALLY, LOU'S DAD WALKS OVER TO US. Dom and I stand up, and my entire body is numb.

"We . . . well, we want to say thanks to you, Graham," Lou's mom says through tears.

"Thanks? To me?"

"I don't think we ever saw her so happy than the time she got to spend with you," Lou's dad says, getting choked up. "She was more like herself these last couple of weeks than she had been in a long time. Maybe ever. We're glad she had that."

"What do you mean *had*?" I ask, my stomach twisting into knots.

"There was clotting," he begins, swallowing a sob. "It went from her legs to her heart and lungs. Where it . . ."

"What?" I say, my brain clouded from too little sleep and too much anxiety. "What does that mean?"

"They tried everything they could. It means we didn't win this one."

He collapses into tears. I've never seen anyone who looks more broken. Dom pats his back.

But me? I'm in the bottom of the sinkhole, where I can't hear anything. Everything is blurry.

Empty.

Hollow.

She can't be gone. She just can't be. We were on the island yesterday, making a fire and running from gigantic alligators. She left me a scavenger hunt. She's okay. She has to be okay.

"We have to remember that because of the same donor other people might get their chance at a miracle today, too. We can't lose sight of that hope," says Lou's mom, looking away.

I feel lightheaded, like I'm shaking. Dom puts his arm around my shoulder.

"We'll be okay," he says quietly.

But it doesn't feel like anything will ever be okay again. Ever.

It wasn't supposed to happen like this. This wasn't how it was meant to be.

FOUND AND LOST

I'M IN LOU'S HIDING PLACE.

I've decided I like it. It's cozy.

I think I'll stay. I'm not ready to face the world yet.

I'm not.

Ready.

I only wish Lou were here with me so she could show me around.

MORNING

"GRAHAM?" I HEAR A VOICE SAY. I OPEN MY EYES AND SQUINT AT THE early sunlight of Monday morning. I fell asleep in the corner of the waiting area last night, but Robb let me move to the chair next to my mom. Some light rule-breaking is just another perk of being the favorite patient, I guess.

"Since we pulled her intubation tube she's been a bit groggy, but your mom will be waking up in a few moments," Robb says. "It'll be good for her to see you first thing."

I wipe the corners of my eyes and sit up in my chair. I feel like I've barely had any sleep. My eyes are bloodshot and tired.

I hold my mom's hand as she slowly starts to stir.

"Graham?" she croaks, her voice barely a whisper.

"Yeah, I'm here. I'm not going anywhere."

Her hands are shaky and she's weak. Her face cringes with pain as she drifts in and out of sleep.

There's a plastic Florida Clinic mug on the stand next to her. Seeing the half-melted ice chunks gives me an idea. One that Lou just gave me.

"Remember how I told you we found the Snail Kite on your island? It was beautiful. Perfect." I reach my hand into my pocket. "I brought back a piece of the island. Remember?"

I pull out a small pinch of sand and hold it in my palm. Mom opens her eyes and lets her fingers brush through the soil as she takes a deep breath in.

"Thank you," she whispers.

I'm so happy I—we—could give this little bit of magic to her. And in an instant, I start to tear up thinking about Lou.

"What is it?" Mom whispers.

I tell her about Lou. How she'd been the one waiting for a transplant. And how she didn't make it.

"Oh no, honey. That's awful," Mom says, tears springing to her eyes.

We sit for a quiet moment.

"You know, I could tell something was going on."

"Really?"

"Give me a little credit, G. She could tell I knew. But you'll always have memories of her. The things you did with each other, the adventures you shared."

"Ha, boy did we have an adventure," I say, wiping away a tear. "Have you ever heard an alligator hiss at you?"

I laugh and cry at the same time. It's weird.

"You'll have to tell me all about it. I can't wait to hear," Mom says. I lean forward and gently hold her hand.

"We'll make it through this, bud. We've come a long way."

She's right. We have. And I know Lou would want me to make the most of my life.

So I plan on it.

My phone buzzes with a message. It's from Dom, and it's a photo. I open it up to see a patch of grass with fresh flowers growing up from it, their petals vibrant and full of life. Then I read the message:

> Remember that bird we buried? It all happens for a reason. (Did I get it right this time?)

WORLDVIEW

LOU'S HIDING PLACE ISN'T LIKE MY WAITING ROOM AT ALL. EVERYTHING'S dark and has more of a feeling of uneasiness throughout it. I've been here for a while now, on the days where I feel like doing nothing.

I call out her name, desperately. "Lou! Louuuuu!" But I'm still alone.

When the worst thing in the world happens, no matter how badly you want it to not be true, it still is.

I can see a hazy light up ahead, so I start walking toward it. As I get closer, I can see it's a tiny window. Like the one that showed up in My Waiting Room when I first met Lou. I stand on my tiptoes and peer through the window.

It's me. And I'm just sitting there. Waiting. Doing nothing.

And then, I feel something tug at my pocket. I reach my hand inside. It's the dirt from the island.

I pull it out and the sand starts to sift through my fingers. And then something extraordinary happens. It falls down to the floor, then starts swirling up like a shimmering vortex. It goes faster and faster, twirling luminescence in every direction. The sand starts clinging to everything it can find.

In an instant, everything changes from a dull dark nothing to a wild, vibrant world. I look up and marvel at the towering trees and the night sky. I look down and I'm standing in a field of sparkling ferns and wildflowers. I can see a pond, with a sinkhole like the one we saw together. Deep from the bottom, there is a glowing gold light.

This world, this hiding space, is the most beautiful place I've ever seen. I know that Lou is here. And she's okay.

Through the window, the lights in My Waiting Room turn off, and everything begins to return to darkness. Lou is telling me it's time to go.

That life is waiting.

And I'm not going to waste any second of it.

A NATURAL

"NOT GONNA LIE, IT'S GOOD TO HAVE YOU BACK, DAVINCI," DOM SAYS FROM the driver's seat of the Blue Beast. I'm sitting next to him in the passenger seat for the first time in weeks. Lately I haven't been sleeping much. Sometimes I feel like that tree that got struck by lightning.

"It's good to be back. Will I get to paint again today?"

"Let's not get carried away," Dom says with a smirk. As we start to back up, I see the side door to the garage open up. Nick runs over to the van and opens the back door.

"Got room for one more?" he says, sliding into the back bench seat.

"Always," Dom says, beaming.

We start the drive toward the jobsite, our noisy van cruising down sparsely traveled back roads. The wilderness of our side of town begins to change as we start passing streets of new homes, their sprinklers drenching bright-green grass. We pass the entrance to Peerless Pines and head toward the worksite for the day.

"Hey, Dad?"

"What's up, bud?" Dom asks. We slowly turn a hill, and Nick's mom's house comes into view.

"Mind if I stop by and say 'hey'?"

The van rolls to a stop in front of the backyard, the engine making a symphony of ticking and clanking noises. Nick opens the back door and hops out.

"Take your time," Dom says from the open window. "You know where to find us."

We watch Nick as he heads to the backyard, opening a gate in the white picket fence. I can't really see anyone through the slits of the white picket fence, but Dom and I can hear contagious laughter.

"Ni-Ni!" shout two tiny voices.

I can see Nick's face above the white fence, and he looks different than I've ever seen him. He looks happy. Very happy.

"You see that? Kids love him," Dom says, putting the van back into gear. "He's a natural."

Dom turns the volume on the radio up, and we rumble forward, toward whatever the day holds for us.

Two Hundred Fifty Words

I'M SITTING IN MY MOM'S NEWEST NEW ROOM, WHICH HAS A VIEW OF PALM trees. It's been almost a month since the surgery, and each and every day there have been fewer and fewer machines and IV drips. It's basically the exact opposite of what we're used to in these hospital rooms. I even overheard doctors saying we might get released this weekend, which would be amazing. Finally putting all this behind us.

I've spent most of my free time at the hospital, so I'm getting pretty good at doing physical therapy with Mom. They've got all these lifts and hoists and things for when you have to relearn a lot of things after the surgery. You know, like walking, breathing. Little stuff.

"G, hand me that lung torture device," Mom says. I hand her the plastic tube that has a little ball inside of it that you lift up with your breath. All the nurses have said it's important to do it a lot, so I've been trying to remind her.

"Did you ever finish the contest entry for the Snail Kite, by the way?" Mom asks me as she does her lung exercises. Mom says she doesn't remember much of anything right after the surgery, which is probably for the best. So I'm surprised she remembers the part of the contest I'd rather forget about.

"Oh. Huh. Guess I sort of forgot about that part," I answer.

It's funny when you have to tell somebody what happened to them even though they were the ones going through it, you know? We'll sit for an hour sometimes, her listening to me trying to fill her in on the details she missed. She does say she remembers the dirt from the island though. Some things are too important to forget.

"Well, let's write it now. I'm just lying around here all day. We can at least say that we sent it in."

"But the contest is already over."

"This one might be only for us," Mom replies. "I'll see if my handwriting is any better today."

She grabs a piece of paper and a pen with the Florida Clinic logo on it.

"And we have two hundred fifty words, right? *'The Snail Kite, by Graham Dodds and Lou Watkins,'*" Mom says as she writes on the paper. Her hand is wobbly, but she's able to hold the pen, which is good. "Now close your eyes. What was it like when you saw it? How did you feel?"

I take a breath.

"Well, I know the first five words at least," I say. "It was meant to be."

BIRD MAIL

"DaVinci, seems like you had some bird mail today," Dom says as he enters the kitchen through the sliding glass door. He tosses a stack of mail on the kitchen counter. "It's from that society."

I guess Mom sent in the entry for me and Lou after all.

"Wow, that's weird. Especially since the contest was over," I say.

But as I check the letter, I can see it's not addressed to me. It's for Nick. What?

"Open it up before we leave for work," Nick says, taking the final slurps of his cereal milk.

"But it's for you."

"I think you should open it. You owe me one, right?"

I open it up and inside is a card with a beautiful picture of a bird on the front.

Dear Nick,

Thank you for your winning entry. Your photo was very candid; it's as if the bird trusts you. We also greatly appreciate you wanting to donate the prize money in your friend Lou's name. In her honor, we've doubled the prize amount for the Children's Wing at the Florida Clinic. Thank you, and happy birding!

A small piece of paper with the Florida Clinic logo falls out of the card: "In memory of Lou Watkins, a rare bird."

VICTORY MILKSHAKE

After a few birding app alerts, I reach into my backpack and pull out the binoculars Lou gave me. It seems like a Mangrove Cuckoo is on the move. Ever since the island, I've carried a bag filled with stuff that I figure would make her proud. Binoculars, a birding guide, waterproof matches, an updated and fully floating map of the marsh, Loretta's lucky hat and patch, and an emergency bag of rice (in case of waterlogged phones).

"And this is, y'all. Four small shakes plus a side of celery," says our server, stopping by the driver's-side window to hand us our bill.

After six months of visits and check-ups, doctors said Mom was allowed one victory milkshake, so naturally we're at Swansen's. This also happens to be the inaugural trip in Dom's new decked-out van. He said it was finally time for a change. It seems Mom isn't the only one with a new motor.

"And what's the name of this new van, Dom?" Mom asks between bites of celery. She's in the passenger seat, while Nick's in the back with me.

He squints, thinking.

"The Blue Beast 2?" he says, taking a sip of his milkshake.

"This thing is green!" Mom says, playfully tossing her crumpled straw wrapper at Dom's head. "We'll keep brainstorming."

I look out through the front windshield of the van and see the trees where my mom collapsed. But the adrenaline and anxiety from before is gone.

"I also want to say I am so grateful for all of you guys," Mom continues.

"And we're grateful for you, Linds. You're a miracle," Dom says, taking a slurp of his shake.

"Well, I couldn't do this alone. But there's something else," she says, fidgeting with the armrest on her seat.

I try not to close my eyes, almost sensing my brain start to panic, beginning to organize all the furniture in My Waiting Room once again. But I take a breath, and I stay right where I am. Ready for whatever news Mom is about to deliver.

"At my appointment today, the doctors said I'm doing really well. So well that we could head back home to Buffalo pretty soon if you want, G."

Dom nervously chews on his straw. Nick turns my way.

It's weird, until recently I've thought of Buffalo as home. Only now . . .

"Mom, what, ah, what if we didn't go back to Buffalo?" I ask her.

"Oh yeah?" she says.

"Yeah. I mean, what would we even do? I'd probably have to make new friends again," I say. "Plus, I make ten bucks an hour down here. And we have a boat—"

"Two boats," Nick says. "And you can even drive mine if you stay here."

"Really?" I ask, surprised.

Mom's face splits into a grin.

"Well then, it's settled," Dom says with a cheesy smile. "Home sweet home."

HELLO. GOODBYE.

I SET MY ICY CUP OF LEMONADE DOWN NEXT TO A BOOK TITLED *YOU, ME, and the Fjords of Norway*. It's the one Lou got from the library. I figured I could read up on them. Maybe my mom and I will even plan a vacation to see them someday.

I'm out on the back porch of the house with the binoculars from Lou around my neck and her friendship bracelet around my wrist. After spotting them a few times, I'm hoping that this pair of Sandhill Cranes might show up. I've learned to never expect them to do anything you'd expect, though, so I'm aimlessly scanning the backyard and listening for new bird calls. Dom claims he saw a Brown Noddy fly past the neighborhood last week, but I'll believe it when I see it.

I also found more of my dad's illustration books in the garage, as well as a blank sketchbook. They've been really helpful as I practice drawing. Plus, it's nice to think I'm helping my dad finish one of his journals.

The first thing I sketched was our Snail Kite, then the Fossil, and then a picture of Lou by the fire. I haven't gotten them quite right yet, but I'm going to keep trying.

I hear the sliding glass door open behind me.

"Dinner's gonna be ready in an hour, Graham. Nick's nearly back from his mom's house," Mom says. "Wow, it's beautiful out, right?"

"Yeah, it really is," I reply, looking up from my book.

It's funny how I used to think of this place as sticky and uncomfortable—scary even. Now, it feels warm and inviting.

"You know, bud," Mom says. "I nearly did a mile on the treadmill at the physical therapy center. I bet I could make it to that canoe of ours with a little more practice."

My eyes go wide. "Really? Are you sure?"

"I am. You know, we still have to name it. That's very bad luck not to, so I've heard."

I nod. "I know, I've been thinking. Is 'Watkins' Wings' too cheesy?"

Mom leans against the doorframe. "It's perfect."

"And maybe the canoe can wait. I'm enjoying not knowing the local EMS teams on a first-name basis," I joke, but only kind of. "How about we do a walk around the block tomorrow? There are some new, fuzzy baby Purple Gallinules that live around the corner. Wanna check 'em out?"

"Deal. I'll be waiting for you tomorrow morning. In the garage. With binoculars and everything. Maybe we can start a new journal together. First entry: the Snail Kite."

My mom shuts the door, and just after that there's a warm

breeze. I see something out of the corner of my eye. A Florida Scrub-Jay lands on the splintered deck railing and looks up at me. I know it sounds ridiculous, but I know in an instant that it's Lou. I remember her saying Scrub-Jays were her favorite bird.

She's here to give me a message. My breath hitches.

"Hi there, Lou," I say, feeling my throat get tight.

She chirps a few scratchy chirps, then hops over to the book about fjords and pecks at its corner.

"Yeah, yeah, I'll make sure I get that back to the library for you," I say with a little chuckle, the lump in my throat getting larger.

Tears start to form in my eyes, but the bird chirps at me, not giving me the permission to sit around feeling sad.

Then it chirps again.

And again.

It nods toward the setting sun, the path leading to the dock, and our island that's somewhere out there in the swamp.

The bird hops toward me and chirps a few more times.

"Okay, okay, I get it," I say with a laugh. I wipe away my tears.

She stays for a while longer with me, both of us enjoying being together once more.

And then, just as the clouds break, she gives another chirp and flies away.

"On to your next adventure," I whisper. "And I'm on to mine."

Acknowledgments

It is my hope that this book might help someone feel seen and understood, as many stories have done for me. I am beyond grateful for the special people who have helped it come to be.

I feel lucky to have had the opportunity to work with everyone at Union Square Kids. Thank you to Tracey Keevan for your openness, compassion, and endlessly impressive birding knowledge, and many thanks to Emily Meehan for the opportunity. Thank you as well to Samantha Knoerzer, Suzy Capozzi, Melissa Farris, Whitney Manger, Renee Yewdaev, and Scott Amerman.

Thanks to Kimberly Glyder for such a beautiful cover design.

I also want to offer my appreciation to the Alloy team for their constant belief and support over the years. To Sara Shandler for your insight and vision, and to Laura Barbiea for your tireless editing efforts. I am very grateful for this journey, and for all the bird-related puns we picked up along the way. Thank you as well to Josh Bank, Les Morgenstein, Joelle Hobeika, and Romy Golan.

And to Hayley Wagreich, thanks for believing in this from the start.

Organ donations save lives, and I want to offer thanks to the medical professionals that were a part of my mom's heart transplant journey.

To Jessica Daniels, for your unending support. To Kay Kendall, for your spirit. To Molly Bolton, for being there. To Dr. Sheffield and Dr. Starling, for working miracles. And to the countless nurses, therapists, and chaplains who were always ready to offer kind words, smiles, or an invaluable laugh.

Fulfilling this dream wouldn't be possible without the loved ones in my life. Thank you, all. To Mom, Dad, Matt and Whitney, for your unwavering support. And to Bridget, for being tough, strong, and kind. And to Igby and Pepper for being terrific feline writing assistants.

Lastly, and perhaps most of all, thank you, dear reader. You really are a rare bird, and don't let anyone tell you otherwise.